THE WORLD BEHIND THE DOOR

THE WORLD BEHIND THE DOOR

DOOR

AN ENCOUNTER WITH SALVADOR DALI

MIKE RESNICK

Watson-Guptill Publications/New York

First published in 2007 by Watson-Guptill Publications, Nielsen Business Media
a division of The Nielsen Company
770 Broadway, New York, NY 10003

Library of Congress Control Number: 2007922230

ISBN-13: 978-0-8230-0416-4
ISBN-10: 0-8230-0416-3

Printed in the U.S.A.

First printing, 2007

1 2 3 4 5 6 7 8 9 / 14 13 12 11 10 09 08 07

Contents

Preface ix

1. Reality Is a Bore 1

2. The Dubious Hypnotic 7

3. Hunting for the Snark 13

4. Jinx 17

5. When the Ludicrous Isn't 25

6. Effect and Cause 33

7. An Angry Figment 43

8. New Perspectives 49

9. The Camembert of Time 57

10. The Greatest Villain 63

11. The Finishing Touch 69

12. The Persistence of Gala 73

13. Wedded Blitz 79

14. Escape 83

15. Big Town   91
16. Alternatives   97
17. Antidotes   101
18. Heisenberg   105
19. Disintegration   113
20. Resurrection   117
    Dali's Life and Art   121
    A Time Line of Dali's Life   125
    For More Information   127

To Carol, as always
And to my daughter, Laura,
Once more, with feeling

Preface

The unusual and the bizarre have always fascinated me. That's probably why I became a science fiction writer.

Science fiction boasts a number of fine writers, but over the years it has had an almost equal number of outstanding artists, artists who could give form and structure to the wildest imaginings of the writers: Frank Frazetta, Michael Whelan, Bob Eggleton, Kelly Freas, Ed Emshwiller, Virgil Finlay, a number of others.

But I persist in believing that the greatest of all science fiction and fantasy artists, even though he never illustrated a science fiction book or magazine, was Salvador Dali.

The first art book I ever bought, back when I was in high school just about half a century ago, was a collection of Dali's paintings. So was the second. And the third. The man's work was so different, so hypnotic, so unlike anyone else's, I just couldn't stop looking at it.

And a lot of it *was* science fictional. What else could you call *The Space Elephant*, or *Dream Caused by the Flight of a Bee Around a Pomegranate One Second Before Awakening*, or *Suburb of the Paranoaic-critical Town*?

It wasn't long before I began studying Dali. How could I not? He himself was as interesting as his paintings. His mustache was longer than most men's beards. His clothing was outlandish, his behavior even more so. His statements were unbelievable—except that when challenged, he often managed to prove that he was telling the truth. He was the world's first great performance artist, long before the term "performance art" even existed.

And that was the key to my fascination. Dali was actually better known than any of his paintings, as famous as *The Persistence of Memory* and the others were. Everyone had heard of Picasso, who was probably the greatest of the modern, twentieth-century artists—but if you were standing next to him in line at the bank or the movie theater, you'd have no idea who he was. The same holds true for Norman Rockwell and every other famous painter of the just-ended century—except for Dali. You'd not only know him if he was standing next to you, you'd know him if you saw him across the street, or two blocks away…and if you *didn't* recognize him, he'd probably do everything short of a striptease to capture your attention in such a way that there could be no doubt of who he was.

His descriptions of himself and his art grew more and more bizarre. It was hinted many times—often by Dali himself—that he was insane. Those who knew him socially were never sure…but those few who worked with him on a daily basis, such as Alfred Hitchcock and Walt Disney, often said the bizarre eccentricities were just an act, that when they were working with him behind closed doors he was a total (and totally sane) professional. Others swear that Dali had pulled the wool over Hollywood's eyes, that his madness came and went and the movie moguls caught him during his very few sane periods.

So which was he?

I didn't know when I started studying him all those years ago, and I don't know today.

But when the nice people at Watson-Guptill asked me to write another book in their Art Encounters series, I jumped at the chance to write about Dali and perhaps find out just how sane or mad he really was. I had done a book on Leonardo da Vinci, who was a scientist, a painter, and an all-around genius; and I'd done one on Toulouse-Lautrec, an embittered and driven man. But I understood both of them, and I understood their work, whereas I would continue to learn about Dali and what inspired his strangest images as I researched and wrote *The World Behind the Door*.

Was Dali sane?

Was he mad?

Was there ever someone like Jinx?

Read the book. Then *you* can tell *me*.

CHAPTER 1

Reality Is a Bore

The elephant stands at least thirty feet high, its huge red body supported on incredibly thin, sticklike limbs.

Dali stares at it, curiously unafraid. There is a howdah on the elephant's back, but it's too far away for him to see who, or *what*, is riding in it. He should be concerned about what kind of creature could tame such an elephant, could bend its will to his own, but instead he finds he is more interested in how the rider got into the howdah. Dali has never seen a ladder that could reach that high. Did the rider fly?

He hears a growl off to his left and turns to look. There is a woman standing there, quite the loveliest woman he has ever seen, wrapped in a thin white shroud that flutters in the breeze. Standing next to her is a huge black-maned lion, glaring at him with baleful, bloodshot eyes.

"I hope he's under your control," Dali says to the woman…or, at least, that is what he *tries* to say. But what comes out is a nursery rhyme:

> "*One, sir, two, sir,*
> *Who are you, sir?*

Three, sir, four, sir,
Tell me more, sir.
Five, sir, six, sir..."

Dali stops. He can't remember the next line, the one that rhymes with "six," and besides, he feels incredibly silly uttering the rhyme in the first place. He decides that it was a momentary aberration and tries again. He opens his mouth to speak, and suddenly gibberish comes out. Well, not *quite* gibberish; at some deep level he knows he is speaking a logical, coherent language, but it is not one that he recognizes. He wonders if he's making any sense at all.

The woman smiles and opens her mouth to answer—but instead of words there is another roar, louder and more frightening than the first one.

"I hope she is not distressing you," says the lion in exquisite Spanish.

Dali stares dumbly at the huge cat.

"I just washed her," continues the lion, "and now I can't do a thing with her."

"Why is she roaring?" Dali manages to say.

"You hurt her feelings by being more interested in the elephant," answers the lion.

"But I didn't know she was here when I saw the elephant," protests Dali.

"Where else would she be?" replies the lion.

"This is sillier than most of my dreams," says Dali. "I've got to wake up."

The lion shrugs. "You can if you can."

"What does that mean?" asks Dali.

The lion begins to answer him, but every time it tries to speak the woman's roars drown it out.

"I guess you'll just have to wake up without my help," apologizes the lion at last, and the woman smiles, yawns, and stretches like a cat.

"Why are all my dreams like this?" asks Dali.

"Like what?" inquires the lion.

"There's no shred of reality in them," he explains, puzzled. "Elephants so tall they could walk right over the Tower of Pisa and not scrape their bellies, rivers that flow upstream, birds that walk and fish that fly, and now a woman who roars and a lion that speaks calmly and rationally. The world is not like this, so why are my dreams?"

"Have you considered the obvious?" asks the lion.

"What do you mean?"

"That what you are experiencing at this moment is reality, and when you sleep, you dream that you are a talented painter whose work shows some promise but is totally derivative."

"No," says Dali firmly. "I *am* a painter. This much I am sure of."

The lion shrugs. "I'm sure I'm a lion."

"No," says Dali. "Lions can't talk."

"You're certain of that?"

Dali nods his head vigorously. "Yes."

"I'm sure I am, you're sure I'm not. One of us must be wrong."

"One of us is," says Dali. "*You* are."

"So I am a mock lion, an ersatz lion?"

"Yes."

"Let us pretend for a moment that you really are a painter, over in that dull country you call reality. Here I am: head, fangs, mane, flanks, loins, claws, tail. How would you paint me to show that I am not a lion?"

Dali stares at the lion for a long moment, considering the question. "I don't know," he admits.

"If you cannot paint the difference between a real and a false lion, what makes you think there *is* a difference?"

"Either something is real, or it is not," insists Dali.

"All right," says the lion. "Paint me. Capture every detail exactly as you see it. When you are done, is the lion in your painting real or not?"

"I don't understand," says Dali, frowning.

"Can it bite you? Can it move? Can it roar?"

"No, of course not. It is just a painting."

"Then it is not real."

"The *painting* is real," says Dali irritably.

"What if you are right, and this is a dream and you have imagined me, and when you wake up you paint the very same picture. Now is it a painting of a real lion?"

"I don't know," admits Dali.

The lion smiles a very human smile. "You see?" he says. "Reality is a lot trickier than you think. We will have to discuss it further."

"Right now?"

The lion shakes his head. "No, right now you are about to wake up. Of course," he continues, "there is the possibility that this is reality, and you will 'waken' into an incredibly boring dream world in which you live in an imaginary country called Spain."

"It is very confusing," says Dali.

"It is more than confusing," says the lion. "It is a conundrum."

"Will anyone ever solve it?" asks Dali, suddenly aware of the pillow beneath his head.

"There is one man who can," says the lion.

"Who is it?" asks Dali. "Will I ever meet him?"

Suddenly, the woman begins laughing. The giggles become wild peels and shrieks as she gasps for breath. Dali wonders what he has said that is so amusing, and finds himself back in his bed, staring at the ceiling of his Madrid apartment.

He gets up, puts on his slippers, pulls his brocaded satin robe around him, and wanders out of the bedroom, past the small kitchen, and into the studio, where he pauses before the easel and surveys the canvas that sits there, clearly a work in progress but far enough along that he knows exactly what the final painting will look like. He is not pleased with it.

There's nothing especially wrong with it; it's just, well, not exactly dull, but…he doesn't know. It lacks something, though he can't put his finger on what's missing.

Probably the best work he has done to date is the painting he has titled *Madrid Slums*. He walks over to where it hangs and studies it. Good lines, good muted colors, very competent composition. Yes, the critics were right: it's good, there's no question of it. His mastery of technique is unquestioned. And certainly a Madrid slum is a more interesting subject than yet another portrait or landscape.

But there is nothing of *him* in the painting, nothing that speaks up and says "This is the unique vision of a man named Salvador Dali, and no one else in the world could possibly have painted it because no one else sees the world in remotely the same way." It's not naturalistic; no one will ever mistake it for a photograph. But no one will ever look at it and say, "Of *course* it's by Dali," either.

Picasso could have painted it in an afternoon, and all the details would be the same, but it would nonetheless be uniquely his own. Dali frowns. Picasso can create twenty paintings a week if he feels like it, and every one of them is clearly by him and no one else. What is the secret? He himself is as unique a human being as Picasso, but his paintings, though well received, don't shout at the world, "I am by Dali and no one else!"

He hasn't admitted it to himself before tonight, but clearly he is trying to, in his dreams.

A strange dream, that one. Strange, but familiar, too, as if he's had it dozens of times, forgetting it each time he awakens, but feeling strangely comfortable every time he falls asleep and revisits that dreamscape.

He shakes his head, as if that will shake off his uncomfortable analysis of his work. It doesn't.

Maybe it's his subject matter, he thinks. Anyone can walk through a slum. Maybe he needs to see things no one else has ever seen, and paint *them*.

But what has no one else seen?

Well, then, maybe he should take the commonplace and turn it into something no one's ever seen. Take his father, for instance. What if he painted a huge spider with his father's face?

He grimaces. He knows exactly what would happen, and there is not the slightest chance that he might live through it.

No, that's not the answer. He's clearly missing something, though. What could Picasso bring to a painting of a Madrid slum that he couldn't? There's no question in Dali's mind that in terms of technique he can match Picasso brushstroke for brushstroke. So what is the real difference?

He has a feeling that if he *knew* the difference, it would show up in his paintings.

Am I just a dull, uninteresting man, he wonders, *destined to paint very well-crafted, dull, uninteresting paintings?*

He doesn't know. He hopes not.

Finally, he shrugs and walks out of the house to enjoy the first rays of the rising run. He stops at a nearby fruit stand, buys a pomegranate, and nods to a couple of bypassers he knows.

Enough self-pity and self-doubt, he thinks. *Tomorrow is a brand-new day, filled with mystery and promise. In fact, here it is tomorrow, and I will spend the entire day painting.*

Well, not the *entire* day, he reminds himself. He has been offered tickets to a lecture by that little man from Vienna, the one whose work continues to stir up so much controversy.

Well, if he gives an interesting talk, maybe I'll offer to paint his portrait, thinks Dali. It's not likely, but one never knows. What was his name again?

Dali searches his cluttered memory. He's read about the man, even discussed him with friends. What in the world was his name?

And finally he remembers.

It is Sigmund Freud.

CHAPTER 2

The Dubious Hypnotic

The two men sat in comfortable leather chairs in a corner of the elegant, wood-paneled hotel bar.

"I appreciate your paying for the drinks, Señor Dali," said Sigmund Freud, taking a sip of his brandy, "but it really wasn't necessary. Your work is not unknown to me. I have been aware of it and admired it for a few years now."

"It is dreck," replied Dali contemptuously, putting a Turkish cigarette into a foot-long jeweled holder and lighting it. "Utter dreck."

"How can you say that?" asked Freud curiously. "You have had several successful exhibitions, you have won some awards, your reputation extends to my own Vienna, and I am told your art brings respectable prices."

"It dabbles on the surface of things," said Dali. "Your lecture this afternoon has opened my eyes. There are worlds undreamed of…and yet I dream of them every night. I thought I might be going mad, and perhaps I still am, but at least I know now that I am not the only one whose nightmares repeat themselves again and again."

"Our dreams are like escape valves," explained Freud, setting his brandy snifter down on the table between them. "When an engine builds up so much steam that it seems it must explode, there will always be a small valve that allows the steam to escape. That is what our dreams do. For example, do you ever dream about your family?"

"How did you know?" asked Dali.

"It's really not at all unusual. Which member dominates your dreams—your father or your mother?"

"Neither."

"Then who?"

"Salvador Dali."

"But that is you."

"It is also my father, but I speak of neither of us." His mouth twitched uncomfortably. "I am not the first Salvador Dali born to my parents. Three years before my birth they had a son, and they named him Salvador. He died before he was two years old." Dali paused, trying to order his thoughts. "I suppose if I behave eccentrically at times, it is to prove that I am me and not that other Salvador, that I am my own unique person."

"And you have been having these dreams for how long?" asked Freud.

"All my life."

"And you have been behaving eccentrically…?"

"All my life."

"And it has seeped over into your artwork." Freud smiled. "I told you: I've seen some of your paintings."

"You know what I think of them," said Dali dismissively. "Yet I am a successful artist, at least in the eyes of the world. I am not hurting for money. No one is threatening my life or my property. Why should I keep having this dream?"

"Perhaps," suggested Freud with a sly smile, "because your work is dreck."

Dali returned his smile. "Perhaps. In fact, that is why I have sought you out. I was wondering: If I were to paint my dream, would *that* become my escape valve? In other words, once I captured it on canvas, would I finally stop dreaming it?"

"This is the dream you were describing to me earlier?" asked Freud.

"Yes."

"The elephant on the stiltlike legs is interesting, though I have no idea how commercial such a painting might be," replied Freud. "But from what you tell me, the main part of your dream concerns a lion that speaks and a pretty girl who growls and roars. How would you create a painting that showed the viewer what makes them the creatures of your dreams, rather than merely a pretty girl and a lion?"

"I don't know," admitted Dali.

"Neither do I," said Freud.

"Then am I never to be free of this dream?"

"Oh, sooner or later it will be replaced by another one," answered Freud. "Probably a much more disturbing one."

"That is not an encouraging answer, Doctor," said Dali unhappily. "You are the foremost authority on the unconscious. If even you cannot help me, then I am doomed."

"May I suggest that you are looking at this all wrong, Señor Dali?" inquired Freud, taking another sip of his brandy.

"I don't understand," said Dali.

"I know you don't," said Freud. "That is why you have come to me."

"Please explain."

"Let me ask you a question first," said Freud. "Are you dissatisfied with just the painting you are currently working on, or with all of them?"

"All of them," answered Dali morosely.

"*Why?*"

"Because it is work anyone could have done."

"Would you consider changing your brushes, or the way you mix your paints?" continued Freud. "Would you paint on wood rather than canvas?"

"No," answered Dali. "It would make no difference."

"Why?"

"Because the end result would look the same, or so similar as to make no difference."

Freud smiled. "Well, there you have it."

Dali frowned in puzzlement. "*What* do I have?"

"The reason for your dissatisfaction. It is not your skill or technique that disappoints you, but your subject matter. You must change what you paint, must find new things, things no one else has ever painted, before you will be free of your particular demons."

"My thoughts exactly!" said Dali enthusiastically. "But where will I find such things? I can travel the world, but whatever I see in Africa or Asia will already have been captured by African and Asian artists."

"Every human being is unique, Señor Dali," replied Freud. "If you can find nothing new in the world, then you must search the inner recesses of your consciousness, your mind if you will, and bring forth those images that are entirely your own, that no one else has ever seen before. And I think you should start with your dream."

"But we've already agreed that I cannot, through my painting, show that the lion can speak and the girl can only roar."

"There will be other dreamlike details, details that you are over-looking," said Freud. "They obviously did not impress you as much, so your conscious mind does not remember them, but if you will consent to hypnosis, they will be revealed, and perhaps they will be proper subjects for your brush and paints. And once we bring them out into the open, there is an excellent chance that your dream will cease." Another smile. "Even if it doesn't, once you have painted all the details, it may seem less strange and upsetting to you."

"And all I have to do is let you hypnotize me?"

"There are no guarantees," answered Freud. "This is the likeliest approach. If it should fail, there are other methods we can try."

"It will fail," said Dali with absolute certainty. "I have too strong a mind. No one can hypnotize me."

Freud laughed aloud. "I have hypnotized more than two thousand men and women, Señor Dali—and every one of them, without exception, told me beforehand that their minds were too strong and that I would never be able to hypnotize them."

"I will be different," said Dali.

"If you say so," replied Freud with no show of concern.

"When do you wish to try?"

"I am in town for two more days," said Freud. "When would it be convenient for you to come to my hotel room?"

"As soon as I finish my cigarette," said Dali promptly. "We might as well get this over with, and then, when you cannot hypnotize me, we can discuss alternatives."

"Very well," replied Freud. "And I shall expect your next painting to be dedicated to me."

"To quote an old saying, be careful what you wish for, Doctor Freud. You may get it."

"I will cherish the knowledge that I helped unlock whatever you have kept bottled up inside you."

Dali finished his drink, waited until Freud had done the same, and put out his cigarette.

"Shall we go?" he asked, leaving some money on the table and getting to his feet.

Freud nodded and stood up. "Follow me, Señor Dali," he said, leaving the bar and walking to elevator, which ascended to the fourth and highest level of the hotel. A moment later, Freud led him to a door and unlocked it.

"A very elegant suite," commented Dali, looking around as he entered. "And a lovely view."

"I must confess I haven't been here long enough to enjoy it. I arrived yesterday in mid-morning. Since then I have given five speeches, and attended both a testimonial dinner last night and a luncheon today." He sighed deeply. "It will be nice to get back home."

"I will accept your being overtired as an excuse," said Dali.

"An excuse?"

"For not being able to hypnotize me," said Dali. "Where do you want me?"

"Where are you comfortable?" asked Freud.

Dali sat down on a plush chair. "Right here."

"Then right there is where I want you," said Freud. "Shall we proceed?"

"By all means," said Dali confidently.

He was in a hypnotic trance in less than three minutes.

CHAPTER 3

Hunting for the Snark

Dali spent the next eight days painting his dream.

And he didn't like it.

The problem, he decided, was that he was doing it from memory, and even with Freud's help he hadn't remembered his dream very well. Yes, there was a lion in it, but somehow it looked exactly like the lion in the zoo, and he was sure that it had seemed distinctive and unique in his dream, but he wasn't sure *how* it had differed from every other lion he'd ever seen.

The same with the girl: she was young, maybe eighteen, and pretty, with dark brown hair and a slim figure. But he'd seen literally hundreds of pretty teenaged girls with dark hair and slim figures; try as he would, he couldn't bring the details to mind that made her different.

The trees were blue. But they branched out exactly like the trees in the park, and their leaves were the same shape, just a different color. Ditto for their bark.

Details. He needed details, and they kept eluding him, slipping through the fingers of his memory. Even Freud hadn't been able to help him remember more.

Still, he was sure Freud was on to something, that all he had to do was find a way to unleash the genius he was sure was trapped inside him, trying to get out. He bought a copy of Freud's popular book, *The Anatomy of Dreams*, and found it fascinating, but couldn't see how to apply it to himself. He even considered making a pilgrimage to Vienna to speak further with Freud while he could still afford it, before the public thought no more of his art than he himself did—but he was still embarrassed by the fact that he'd been hypnotized so easily, and couldn't confront the Austrian this soon.

Amazing, thought Dali. *I am capable of the most outrageous acts to publicize myself and my paintings, but I cannot force myself to visit a man I revere, a man who considers me a friend, because I feel I have made a fool of myself in front of him. No wonder he finds the study of human behavior so endlessly fascinating.*

Still, that didn't mean he couldn't use Freud's advice, and possibly even his methods. So he spent the day trying to bring up odd and unusual images, but he was not Freud, and he wasn't trained in the science that Freud had pioneered. He felt that some vital part of him was missing, and he didn't know how to find it or get it back.

Well, he told himself, *maybe instead of sitting here feeling sorry for myself, I should be out looking for it.*

But since I don't know what it is, how will I know where to look for it?

Half the fun of finding something is searching for it, he answered himself silently. *And who knows what you'll find along the way? Surely you can't look into every nook and cranny of your life and not find things to paint.*

But this…this thing I'm looking for, this mystical missing part of me—will I know it when I find it?

What do you care? he answered. *If you find it, your audience will know, and isn't that all that counts?*

"I suppose so," said Dali out loud. "But it certainly sounds like a quest for Lewis Carroll's mythical Snark, a creature that appears in different guises to different people."

He went to his closet, pulled out his coat, and left the house to begin walking through town, not quite sure what he was looking for. He saw two drunks fighting outside a tavern, which was interesting but hardly unique. He passed a brothel, which was interesting *and* (he had to admit) exciting, but even less out of the ordinary than the fistfight. Soon he passed the arena, and considered it for a moment. After all, he was a Spaniard, and if there was one thing Spaniards loved, it was watching the matadors face the brave bulls on the sun-baked sand of the arena.

Suddenly, he shook his head vigorously. *Every* Spanish artist painted the bulls. That was the best reason he could think of *not* to paint them.

Is it Madrid? he wondered. Hemingway and others were producing brilliant literature and art living in Paris on the Left Bank. Maybe he should consider moving there. Or perhaps even America—Babe Ruth and Valentino and the leftovers from the recently concluded Roaring Twenties. It didn't take him long to reject the idea: those were all *external* stimuli, and he knew the problem was within him.

Eventually, he found himself walking past a fish market, and a crab, imported from the coast, caught his eye. It was most unusual thing he'd seen in days, with its awkward eyestalks, its armored pincers, free from all the restrictions of Dali's world, capable of acts of murder and cannibalism in the course of a normal day. It was fascinating—and yet, and yet…it was still just a crab. Interesting, fascinating, even…but anyone who saw it could paint it, and there were a handful of artists who could paint it every bit as well as he could.

He sighed, realized that he was starting to shiver from the cold night breeze, and began walking home. When he arrived, he took off his coat, went over to the closet, and hung it up—and froze, frowning.

"I never saw that before," he muttered, staring at the door in the back of the closet. "I wonder if it leads to a storage room I didn't know was there?"

There was only one way to find out, so he reached out, grabbed the knob, turned it, and stepped through.

And found his Snark.

CHAPTER 4

Jinx

"Where am I?" muttered Dali as he surveyed his surroundings.

He was no longer inside, but out in the open—but not the open of Madrid, or even the Spanish countryside. It was an alien landscape, half dream and half nightmare. Trees were upside down, their branches and leaves in the ground, their roots reaching for the sun. Off to his left was a small waterfall—but the water was flowing *up*. A bird flapped its wings but couldn't take off, while a tree snake glided effortlessly through the air from one tree to another one some fifty feet away.

"I'm dreaming again," said Dali. "I suppose to wake up I must go back through the door."

He turned and looked for the door, but there was no door, no closet, nothing familiar at all.

"Well," he said aloud, "as long as I'm thinking clearly, I might as well explore my dreamscape. Who knows? Maybe Freud was right; maybe there is something here I can incorporate in my paintings."

"Maybe there is," agreed a chipmunk that was standing right next to his foot.

"A talking chipmunk!" exclaimed Dali. "I don't remember dreaming of one before. Remarkable!"

"A talking man!" said the chipmunk. "What will they think of next?"

The chipmunk wandered off in search of food.

"Don't go away yet!" said Dali urgently.

The chipmunk turned and looked at him expectantly.

"Where am I?" asked Dali.

"You are here," said the chipmunk. "And if you walk forty-three feet to your left, you will be there."

"What is this place called?"

The chipmunk stared at him curiously. "Why would you want to call it anything? It won't answer, you know."

"All places have names," said Dali.

"Silliest thing I ever heard," said the chipmunk. "Next you'll be telling me that effect *follows* cause."

"Doesn't it?"

"It depends on the time of day, the day of the week, and whether or not it's raining," answered the chipmunk. "Now, have you any other foolish questions to ask before I catch my lunch?"

"Yes."

"Why am I not surprised?" replied the chipmunk in goading tones. "All right, go ahead and ask it. But just one. You're ruining my appetite."

"How do I wake up?"

"You open your eyes."

"But they *are* open."

"Then you're awake."

"What use are you?" asked Dali disgustedly.

"That's another question, and I only agreed to answer one." With that the chipmunk took a deep breath, plumped up like a balloon, and floated away.

Dali stood still and considered his situation. If this was a dream, it was more realistic and detailed than any he could remember, but it was just as illogical.

And if it's not a dream? he wondered. Then it meant that he had gone over the edge, and he might *never* find his way out of this…this whatever-it-was.

He didn't know what to do. He wished he had his sketch pad, so he could draw some of the strange things he saw, but all he had in his pockets was a pencil, nothing to draw upon.

Then he noticed a white birch tree a few yards away, and he walked over to it. He knew that if one peeled the bark away, it could be written on, and if it could be written on, then surely it could be drawn on.

He reached out, found a small loose section, and gently pulled at it.

"*Ouch!*"

"Who said that?" demanded Dali, looking around.

There was no answer.

He stood still for a full minute, scanning the area, but couldn't find any sign of the speaker. Finally he decided that it had been nothing but his overwrought imagination, and he concentrated on the bark, tugging at it again.

"Damn, that smarts! Do I go around pulling off your skin?"

Dali stared disbelievingly at the tree. "You said that?"

"Of course I said that."

"I've got to get out of here!" said Dali.

"Just like a human," said the tree. "No apology, no remorse, no thought for the discomfort you've caused me. Your only thought is for yourself."

"But you're just a figment of my imagination," protested Dali.

"Do you really think so?" asked the tree curiously. "I could have sworn you were a figment of mine."

"Stop teasing him," said a feminine voice. "Can't you see he's a stranger here?"

Dali spun around, fearful of what he might confront, but he found himself facing a rather pretty girl, barely in her teens. Her hair was bright red, shoulder length, with a little swirl at the end of it, and she wore a yellow satin bow in it. Her face was lightly freckled, her eyes a clear blue, her nose on the small side. She wore a plaid dress that came down halfway between her knees and her ankles, and she had a bracelet of some bone-like material Dali had never seen before.

"You look…real," he said lamely.

"I am real," she replied. She extended a hand. "My name is Jinx. Please don't be mad at my tree. It was just having a little fun with you."

Dali stared at her hand but seemed afraid to touch it, to find out that she was something other than the young girl she seemed to be. "But I should make amends," he said. "After all, I hurt it."

"Not a bit," answered Jinx. "It doesn't feel pain. If you really want to upset it, tell it how pretty the maple tree over there is."

Dali made no reply, but just stood there silently, trying to absorb what he was experiencing.

"Why are you staring at me?" asked Jinx. She quickly ran her fingers lightly over her face. "All the pieces are here—eyes, nose, mouth, ears." She suddenly looked worried. "Is there more? Am I missing something?"

"No," said Dali. "You're the first normal thing I've seen here."

"Normalcy can be a pretty tricky thing, you know," said Jinx. "For example, normal dress at a nudist camp isn't normal dress at a high tea. And speaking of normal, it's not normal to go around pulling the bark off trees. Are you *that* hungry?"

"I'm not hungry at all," answered Dali. "I didn't want to eat it; I wanted to draw on it. I am an artist."

Suddenly, her face came alive with interest. "You are?" she said enthusiastically. "*I* am an artist, too! What is your name?"

"Salvador Dali."

"May I call you Salvador?"

"Please do."

"Do you have any of your art with you, Salvador?"

Dali shook his head. "No. I don't know how I got here, or even where I am. All my art is back in my studio."

"May I see it?"

"If you can show me how to get back, you can *have* some of it," said Dali.

She stared at him as if considering her next statement. Finally she spoke.

"If I show you how to get back, indeed how to come and go whenever you want, will you give me lessons?"

"It's a bargain!" said Dali eagerly. He was about to extend his hand to shake on it, but at the last moment he thought better of it. "This is a very unusual place you live in," he continued after a moment. "Everything is so strange here."

"Not as strange as my paintings," said Jinx.

"Birds walk, snakes fly, rivers flow upstream, chipmunks and trees talk…what could be stranger than that?"

"There's nothing strange about that," replied Jinx. "It's the natural course of things. If you want strange, you should see my art. It upsets everyone who sees it."

"That's not a terrible thing," said Dali.

"It isn't?"

"At least they remember it. If it's unique, if no one else paints like it, then it will always be identified with you."

"Is that a good thing?" asked Jinx.

"Do you want to just be another painter, interchangeable with all your peers?" said Dali. "Or do you want your work to stand out, to be like no one else's?"

"It already stands out, and nobody except me understands it," said Jinx.

Dali smiled. "I feel an affinity with you, Jinx. I don't know where I am or how I got here, but I'm glad we met, and I hope the next time I fall asleep or get drunk I meet you again."

"You won't, you know," said Jinx.

"Oh?"

She shook her head. "When you sleep, you dream. I am not a dream. You can visit me whenever you want, and I hope you will let me visit you, but only when you're awake."

"You're sure I'm awake?"

"Yes."

"It *is* the middle of the night, though," he continued, looking at his wristwatch. Suddenly he noticed Jinx staring at his watch in rapt fascination. "What is it?" he asked.

"I've never seen anything like it before," she said.

"You've never seen a watch?"

"I've seen lots of watches. But never one like that."

"I don't understand," said Dali.

"It doesn't change."

He held it out for her. "The hands move."

"But the watch doesn't change. It's fixed and rigid. It was flat and circular a minute ago, and I suspect it will be flat and circular an hour from now."

"Of course it will."

"That's what's so strange. The world changes with each passing second. I have never heard of a watch that didn't change too, to show the passage of time."

"You are a very interesting young lady," said Dali. He smiled. "And a very pretty one, with just the right number of eyes and noses."

"Thank you," she said. "If you like, I will pose for you." She paused. "But I won't take my clothes off."

"I haven't asked you to."

"But you would have. All artists like to see what's beneath the clothing. I would disappoint you: just arms and legs. No snakes, no insects, no white bones."

"Good God!" exclaimed Dali. "What do the people of this world look like?"

"It's your world, too, you know," said Jinx. "And they look just like people."

"I am losing my mind," he said. "For a few minutes there everything seemed to make sense, but clearly I have gone over the edge."

"The edge of what?" she asked curiously.

"Of sanity."

"I think I had better take you home, Salvador, before you convince yourself that you've gone mad." She reached out and took him by the hand. "Come this way."

She walked ten paces to the left, then ten to the right. Then she led him in a large circle.

"But we're right back where we started," said Dali, puzzled.

"Do you really think so?" asked Jinx.

"It's obvious," said Dali.

"Then why are you standing next to the door at the back of your closet?"

He turned and was astonished to find the door, standing all by itself, about ten feet from the birch tree. He reached out tentatively, half expecting it to be an illusion, and his hand made contact with the knob.

"It's a door!" he whispered in awe.

"Of course it is," said Jinx. "I told you I'd take you back to your home."

He opened it, stepped through, and found himself standing in his closet. "Come along," he said to Jinx, waiting for her to join him before closing the door.

"This is a very strange place," said Jinx.

"In what way?" asked Dali.

"The rooms are square, the walls are straight, and all the rooms have ceilings," said Jinx, frowning in puzzlement. "It's like a very weird dream."

"It is?"

"Absolutely," she said. "I'll bet your chair doesn't even talk to you."

"No, it doesn't."

"And the rug—why is it so big?"

"To cover the floor," said Dali.

"Is the floor that ugly?"

"No."

"Then why don't you have a little rug, maybe the size of a pillow?" she asked. "You could just order it to keep moving under your feet whenever you walked, so you wouldn't have to walk on the wood floor unless you wanted to."

Dali had been listening intently. Finally, he smiled.

"Can I get you something to eat or drink?" he asked solicitously. "I have a feeling we've got a lot to talk about."

CHAPTER 5

When the Ludicrous Isn't

Dali prepared tea for Jinx and poured himself a glass of wine from two different bottles, one red, one white.

"Why do you drink that?" she asked, indicating his rosé-colored wine, when he rejoined her in the studio. "It can't taste very good."

"I drink it because no one else does."

"But maybe there is a reason why no one else does," she persisted.

"Reason and consistency are the twin hobgoblins of little minds," he replied disdainfully. "I do not smoke my cigarettes through a twelve-inch holder because it makes them taste better, or because it is easy to manipulate. I do it because it adds to all the things that make me Dali." He paused. "I do many such things. Once, when I saw the carcass of a bat in the park, I ran over, picked it up, and took a bite, just to see what it tasted like."

"How could that possibly help you as a painter?"

"I must experience things than no one else experiences if I am to paint things no one else paints."

"It sounds good," she admitted. "But I really don't see the connection."

"You are very young."

"Will a dead, rotting bat taste better when I am older?" asked Jinx.

"I do these things to be regarded with awe, not to be imitated," said Dali.

"I thought you painted to be regarded with awe."

"That, too," he said. "You've had a few minutes to look at them. What do you think?"

"These are good," she said, indicating his two most recent efforts.

"Thank you," said Dali, surprised that he actually cared about a young girl's opinion—and such a strange girl from such a strange place. To his surprise, he briefly found himself wondering if she was even real.

"Yes," she said. "Nice use of color. Excellent brush strokes. They are very good first efforts."

"I beg your pardon!" said Dali heatedly.

"Why?" she asked innocently. "They don't offend me. They show great promise." She paused. "I wish I knew why men had such an overwhelming urge to paint naked women."

"Suppose you tell me what's wrong with them." said Dali, trying to control his temper.

"With naked women?" she asked.

"With the paintings."

"Don't you know?" asked Jinx.

Dali stared at the paintings, and all the energy seemed to leave him. He slumped down on a chair, deflated. "Of course I know," he said. "They are exquisite examples of the mundane. They are fine displays of the current state of painting on the European continent, and they could have been painted by any of fifty men I could name."

"See?" she said with a smile. "You *do* know."

"Knowing what's wrong is a far cry from knowing how to improve them," said Dali unhappily.

"True," she said. "But it's a first step—and like they say, every journey begins with one."

"I am already in my twenties," he replied. "If it has taken me this long to take one step, how am I ever to achieve anything of lasting value?"

"Maybe we can help each other," suggested Jinx. "Maybe while I am learning from you, you can learn from me."

"But you're just a child."

"Perhaps I am," she admitted. "But I knew what was wrong with your paintings, and I am sure you will know how to help me become a painter."

"Let me ask you a question," said Dali.

"Ask anything you want."

"Why do you want to become a painter?"

She considered her answer for a moment, then spoke: "Part of it is because art *lasts*. If I am a good painter, people will admire my work long after I am dead, and I find that comforting." Suddenly, a guilty smile crossed her freckled face. "But I suppose the real reason is that painting makes me happy. Not just putting colors on a piece of canvas, but painting something that's meaningful to me, that would never have been painted quite that way by anyone else. *That* makes me happy."

"You are wise beyond your years, young Jinx," said Dali admiringly.

"Why do you paint, Salvador?"

"I am not totally sure," he replied. "I paint to make money, of course, and to become famous, but that is a given. I think the real reason I paint is perhaps the exact opposite of yours. You wish to capture the images of things that are unique to you; I wish to expunge them from my soul, and capture them on canvas, with everything the word 'capture' implies. Once there, they cannot invade my subconscious again. Or at least that is what my friend Freud would say."

"But I sense you also want to be the best," she said. "That you are unhappy with anything less than brilliance."

"Of course," agreed Dali, pacing restlessly around the studio. "With proper training, *anyone* can become a painter. But to become an *artist*…"

"You have it within you, Salvador," said Jinx. "I can tell that from what little I've seen of your work."

Dali stared at her long and hard, then sighed deeply. "Why am I listening to a girl who is barely in her teens?"

"Because no one else has told you what you need to hear," said Jinx with a smile.

"My friend Lorca, the writer, once told me what he thought I needed to hear," said Dali. "Do you know how I responded?"

"No."

"I shaved my head, buried my hair on the beach, and didn't speak to him again for years."

"You've gone out of your way to appear so strange and eccentric that everyone except Señor Lorca probably thought you'd start foaming at the mouth if they spoke to you frankly."

"Perhaps," said Dali, not without a trace of satisfaction. Suddenly, he glanced nervously around the studio and out into the adjoining room. "What am I to do with you?"

"Teach me and learn from me."

He grimaced. "That is not what I meant. I have this…ah…*friend*…"

"Your mistress?" asked Jinx curiously.

"Not exactly," said Dali uncomfortably. "She is a married woman."

"Then what does it matter if she sees me here?"

"It could become awkward," said Dali. "We have an…understanding. As soon as I am more successful, she will leave her husband and marry me. But in the meantime…" He let the sentence linger in the air for a moment. "She has a temper, and she is *very* possessive."

"If she loves you," said Jinx, "why does she not leave her husband now?"

"You are just a child," answered Dali, suddenly very uncomfortable, because he could think of a number of reasons why Gala didn't leave her husband, each of them valid, and each very unflattering to Dali. "You do not understand."

"I understand *love*," she replied, "and if you ask me—"

"I didn't and I won't," interrupted Dali. "The subject is closed."

"What is her name?" she asked, ignoring his order.

"Gala."

"It is a pretty name."

"She is a pretty woman. In fact, she is a beautiful woman. There will come a time when I will include her face in every painting I do."

"That sounds very tedious."

"That is because you have not seen her," said Dali. "At night in the summer, we would walk along the beach near her seaside villa, and every few steps I throw myself on the sand and kiss her feet."

"You must love her feet very much," said Jinx.

Dali sighed. "You make it sound ludicrous."

"*I?*" asked Jinx, unable to repress a smile of amusement.

Dali sighed. "All right. *I* make it sound ludicrous. But it isn't."

"Say that again."

"Why?" asked Dali, puzzled.

"Because that's the answer," said Jinx.

"What are you talking about?"

"The ludicrous doesn't appear ludicrous to you."

"So?"

"So think about it," she said.

He stared at her, puzzled. "You look like you think you've said something profound, but I have no idea what you're talking about."

"Then that's doubtless why you haven't painted it yet."

"Painted *what*?" he asked irritably.

"May I have some more tea, please?" she replied sweetly, holding out her cup.

"You are making no more sense than the crazed world behind the door in the back of the closet!" snapped Dali, so annoyed that he couldn't hold the pot steady and spilled some tea on the floor after filling her cup to the brim. He put the pot in the kitchen before he made an even bigger mess, then returned to the studio.

"No more and no less," she said.

"All right," he said in frustration. "Now what does *that* mean?"

"It means that if you know how to make your way through my world, it makes perfect sense, and if you would listen to me, you would see that *I* make perfect sense, too."

Dali glared at the young redhead, half-admiring her calm and air of certainty, half-enraged by it.

"You seem very sure of yourself, young lady."

"Thank you."

"Thank you for what?"

"For calling me a young lady," replied Jinx, brushing a wisp of hair back from her face. "No one's ever done that before."

"Could we get back to the subject, please?" said Dali, trying to hold his exasperation in check.

"Certainly."

He paused, and his face went blank. "Suddenly, I'm totally confused. What *was* the subject?"

"The answer to your problem." She paused. "Your problem as a painter, not your problem with Gala's feet."

"I have no problem with her feet."

"With the rest of her, then."

"Leave her out of this and tell me the answer to my problem as an artist," he said, picking up his wine glass and downing its contents with a single swallow, then grimacing at the terrible taste.

"I already told you," explained Jinx patiently, "but you weren't paying attention."

Dali began pacing back and forth in front of her.

"Tell me again."

"You said it yourself," replied Jinx.

He stopped in his tracks. For just a moment it seemed he was about to scream at her, or perhaps even take a swing at her, but through an enormous effort of will he forced himself to become calm.

"*What* did I say?"

"That the ludicrous doesn't appear ludicrous to you," she answered.

Dali was silent for a long moment, lost in thought. "So you are saying that I should paint the ludicrous?" he asked at last. "That I paint the things I see in my dreams—or the world behind the door in the closet?"

"It would be unique, wouldn't it?"

"It would be ridiculous!"

"Only if you thought you were painting something ridiculous," she said. "May I give you an example?"

"Please do."

"All right," said Jinx. She lowered her head in thought for a few seconds, then looked up. "Imagine a roly-poly animal with six legs and three eyes, the size of a small dog, but more closely resembling a pig. Pretend it is blue, and that it is somewhat cross-eyed. That's ridiculous, is it not?"

"Certainly."

"Now imagine the same animal, its breasts filled with milk, mournfully nudging the corpse of its dead baby. Is it still ridiculous?"

"No, it is not."

"But it is the same animal," said Jinx. "You see? If the artist does not think it is ridiculous, he will not paint its image in such a way that it appears ridiculous."

Dali sat down heavily and remained motionless for almost a full minute. Finally, he looked up at Jinx.

"You have a point," he admitted. Then: "How many other artists have entered your world?"

"The only entrance is in your closet, Salvador," she replied. "How many artists have you ushered through the door?"

"I never even knew it existed until tonight."

"Then you know the answer."

"So I am the only one to see it?" he persisted.

"Except for the people who live there," said Jinx. "Just as I am the only one from the other side of the door to see *your* world." Suddenly, she giggled. "They will think me quite mad when I finally paint it."

Dali said nothing, and after a moment Jinx spoke again.

"What is the matter, Salvador?"

"I am still considering it," he said.

"Teaching me to paint?" she replied. "We have an agreement."

"I will teach you to paint," he said distractedly. "I am considering what you said."

"Why?" she asked. "You know I'm right."

"Are you this bold at home, young lady?" he asked.

"I prefer to think of it as self-confidence."

"I assume that is an affirmative?"

"Yes."

"Has anyone told you that you are an exceptionally precocious young lady."

"I do not know that word," said Jinx. "Is it a good thing or a bad thing to be?"

"That all depends."

"On what?"

"On whether or not my painting improves," said Dali.

"Then you're going to follow my advice?" she asked happily.

He drew himself up to his full height. "I am going explore your suggestion," he replied with dignity.

"Same thing," said Jinx.

Dali seemed about to lose his temper. Then, instead, he smiled.

"Same thing," he agreed.

CHAPTER 6

Effect and Cause

Three days had passed, days in which Jinx worked on her sketchbook and Dali on a painting. Neither showed the other what they had done, preferring that the other see only the finished creation.

The young girl had filled almost every page in her sketchbook. What she lacked in skill and polish, she made up for in enthusiasm. Everything fascinated her: the walls and ceiling, the floors, the sink in the kitchen, the tile on the floor of the bathroom, the dogs and cats that wandered into sight as she looked out the window. None of her finished sketches pleased her, but the mere act of sketching gave her enormous pleasure. She thought she could see improvement, however minimal, from one day to the next, and that kept her spirits up.

She slept in a spare room. It may have been meant as a guest room when the architect designed it, but it was filled to overflowing with paints, canvases, sketchbooks, easels, chalk, pencils, all the tools of the artist's trade. She was surprised not to be sharing the room with a bowl filled with fruit and a nude model.

Jinx decided that Dali's cooking was all but inedible, so he finally agreed to take her to one of his favorite tavernas. He had feared that he would get a lot of knowing glances—looks that said *Dali has a new mistress! We must tell Gala of this!*—but the streets were relatively empty, and the few people he passed paid him no attention at all.

When they reached the taverna, they seated themselves. There was no menu, of course. The table had a garish cloth over it, and an old wine bottle held two limp flowers. They sat in splendid isolation for a few minutes, and then Jinx got to her feet.

"I must excuse myself for a moment," said Jinx, heading off toward the single bathroom.

Dali nodded absently, briefly considered eating the flowers and drinking the dirty water from the wine bottle, but rejected the notion when he realized that there was no one else in the taverna. No sense acting like a crazy man if there was no one around to appreciate it and report it to their friends.

The waiter brought out the meals—there was no point in ordering a particular dish, since the taverna only cooked one dish per day—and stopped to chat with Dali for a moment.

"You have a guest today, Señor Dali?" he asked, indicating the chair that had clearly been moved when Jinx got out of it.

"My cousin from Barcelona," lied Dali.

"How goes the painting?"

"The same as usual, Felipe," said Dali. "What have we for dinner?"

"Today's catch."

"That's what you had the last five times," said Dali. "When are you going to serve something interesting?"

"I can speak to my uncle, who does the cooking," said Felipe. "What did you have in mind?"

"Robins' beaks, chocolate-covered cicadas, black mamba imported from Africa."

Felipe chuckled. "You are always making the jokes, Señor Dali."

"You get them, I will eat them."

"You know, I almost believe you would." Still chuckling, he vanished back into the kitchen just before Jinx returned to the table.

Jinx ate her meal enthusiastically, but Dali kept glancing at the door, wondering just how many of his bones Gala would break if word of his new companion reached her. He figured the odds against her believing that Jinx was just a student and a friend were about the same as the sun turning into a snowball before morning.

They finished the meal. Jinx went outside while Dali pulled some bills out of his pocket and laid them on the table.

"Thank you, Señor Dali," said Felipe, emerging from the kitchen at the sound of Dali's chair being pushed back. He looked around. "Your cousin never showed up."

"My cousin is outside waiting for me." Dali indicated Jinx's empty plate. "You can see that she ate her dinner."

"I can see that *somebody* did," said Felipe, sure Dali was making some kind of joke. "I'll tell my uncle that you enjoyed his cooking twice as much as usual. And I'll make sure he prepares frosted walrus whiskers the next time you come by."

Felipe laughed uproariously at his own joke and vanished again back into the kitchen.

"It was a nice meal," said Jinx as Dali joined her outside the taverna. "But next time we go out for dinner, I want to go someplace big and crowded. It would be more interesting and exciting."

"We'll see," said Dali noncommittally, for he had already decided that it made more sense to go places like this taverna, where there was no one to report him to Gala.

"You are afraid of Gala," she said suddenly.

"I am not!" he lied, startled.

"We can go to some restaurant or taverna where nobody knows you, and then they will not tell her."

"There is no place where I am not known," said Dali, not without a touch of pride. "If I see a new woman, or create a new painting, or even lose a wager, they know about it almost as soon as it happens. It is the price of fame. You know," he added, lowering his voice confidentially, "I was kicked out of art school when I declared that none of my professors had the skill and knowledge to properly evaluate my work." He grinned. "*That* story made the rounds, I can tell you. They *still* talk about it."

"You look very proud of yourself," noted Jinx.

"I am."

"May I ask you a question?"

"Certainly."

"What did it accomplish, except to get you kicked out of school and convince everyone that you were a pompous, conceited, ill-mannered egomaniac?"

He stared at her in surprise. "No one has spoken to me like that since I was a child."

"Maybe they're afraid of you," suggested Jinx.

"And you are not?"

"Why should I be?" she replied calmly. "I know you're not going to hit me."

"Maybe I won't teach you how to paint."

She smiled at him. "And maybe the next time you visit my world I won't show you how to get back to this one."

"Do you always speak like this to grown-ups?" said Dali.

"Only when I must," said Jinx. "Now, what about my suggestion?"

"What suggestion?" he asked, puzzled.

"That we go to a restaurant where you are not known," answered Jinx.

"I told you—"

"I know what you told me," she said. "But there are thousands of restaurants in Madrid. I refuse to believe that you have graced each and every one of them with your presence. Do you know what I think?"

"What?" asked Dali.

"I think you just do not want to go anywhere where people don't know who you are."

"Perhaps," he said with a shrug.

"If you someday become a great artist instead of merely a very good painter, you will not be able to go anywhere in the world without people knowing who you are," she said. "You might consider that."

"You are very young and innocent of the world," said Dali. "The only artist of the past half century anyone but his friends and associates could identify was little Henri Toulouse-Lautrec, not because he was a great painter, but because he was a physical freak."

"You will find a way," said Jinx with certainty.

"You really think so?" asked Dali, interested. "Why?"

"Because you are a pompous, conceited egomaniac."

"That again," he said. "Do you take a certain delight in insulting me?"

"I wasn't insulting you," said Jinx.

"Oh?" he said, arching an eyebrow. "Is that what you consider praise?"

"I wasn't insulting you *or* praising you," said Jinx. "I was *defining* you. You are an egomaniac—and an egomaniac will find ways to make himself noticed."

"Perhaps you think I should cut myself off at the knees like the little Frenchman?" he replied sarcastically.

"No," she said seriously. "You are not the type to copy someone else. That's what you don't like about your painting; that it isn't uniquely your own. You will cultivate some physical feature or mannerism that no one else possesses, so that when people see it they will say, 'Why, who else could that be but Salvador Dali?'"

"I could shave my head bald," he suggested, half-seriously.

"There have been other bald artists."

"Then what?"

She shrugged. "I don't know. But you will think of something. It is your nature to be the center of attention."

"What do you know about my nature?" he asked. "I've known you for less than half a week."

"All right," she said with a shrug. "I was wrong. You hate the limelight and wish only to be ignored."

Dali couldn't repress an amused laugh at that. "All right, young Jinx. I take it back. Of course you know my nature, and you are absolutely right. Now if you truly know how to turn me into the artist I long to be, I shall forsake Gala's face and put yours into every painting."

"I'd rather you didn't," said Jinx.

"Why?"

"Because not everyone longs to be the center of attention," she explained. "All I want is to be the best artist I can be. I don't care if I receive any acclaim or notoriety; I just want to know that I have made the most of my gifts, however modest they may be."

"That is a very unusual attitude," commented Dali, "and a very mature one. Most of the painters I know would much rather be famous than good."

"I suspect that's true of writers and actors as well," said Jinx.

"The odd part is that the ones who are good are usually the ones who become famous," continued Dali. "An American president once said that you can't fool all of the people all of the time, and indeed you can't—because eventually they realize that, as in Hans Christian Anderson's fable, the emperor has no clothes. That's why I will personally take care of the notoriety, but only to draw attention to my work—and if my art isn't exceptional, then as quickly as I make people seek it out, they will lose interest and look elsewhere."

"May I see what you've done so far on the current one?" asked Jinx.

Dali shook his head. "Not until it's done."

"When will that be?"

"There are two answers to that," he replied. "The first is: Sometime tomorrow. The second is: Never."

"They are both good answers."

Dali paused for a moment. "Are you getting tired?" he asked solicitously.

"A little," she replied. "What time is it?"

He looked at his watch. "Almost ten o'clock."

"Already? How time flies!"

Dali shook his head. "Time doesn't fly. It lays there like a sodden
beast."

"I've never seen a sodden beast."

"Then we're even," he replied. "I've never seen time fly. Shall we begin
walking back to my place?"

"Yes, I think so," agreed Jinx.

"You have been asking me questions all week. Allow me to ask you
one: Why are you called Jinx?"

"Don't you like it?"

"It's very distinctive," he answered. "I've never met anyone else called
Jinx. But I have encountered the word many times, so my question really
is: Who did you jinx?"

"My father," she said.

"He wanted a son?"

"He wanted my mother. She died when I was born."

"I can sympathize," said Dali. "We had some early tragedy in our
family, too."

"I keep explaining that it wasn't my fault my mother died," she said.
Suddenly a tear ran down her cheek. "But it probably was."

"You mustn't blame yourself," said Dali. He wanted to reach out, to
put his arms around the young girl, to hold her close to him and comfort
her—but some instinct prevented him from touching her. Maybe he was
afraid he'd find out he didn't love Gala as much as he thought; he didn't
know. He just knew that he shouldn't touch her. "I had an older brother

who died just before I was born. They gave me his name—and because of that I've always felt that I was a substitute, that I could never live up to the original." He smiled ruefully. "Isn't that foolish? My brother died at twenty-one months of age. How could I not live up to that?"

"You can't control your secret beliefs and fears," said Jinx, as they turned onto a winding side street filled with centuries-old stone buildings, their heels clicking on the ancient brick pavement.

"Freud says you can." He paused. "I would like to believe him. But I don't know if I do."

"Poor Salvador," she said, as another tear followed the first down her freckled cheek.

"Don't move!" he said suddenly.

"What is it?" she asked nervously. "Is it a rat?"

"No," said Dali, pulling his sketch pad out of his pocket. "It is that sad expression that seems to encompass all the troubles of the world. I must capture it!" He positioned himself beneath a gas street lamp and sighed deeply. "It's gone."

"You shouldn't have frightened me."

He began drawing rapidly, "Let me see if I can approximate it before I totally forget what it looked like."

His hand moved faster and faster, becoming a blur of motion. In less than a minute, he stopped and looked up at her.

"I lost it," he said unhappily. "Next time I tell you not to move, don't move."

"May I see it?" she asked, extending her hand.

"It's not very good."

"I'd like to see it anyway," she said. "After all," she added with a half-smile, "I posed for it. Sort of."

"All right, but don't judge it too harshly," he said apologetically. "It's just a spur-of-the-moment sketch, and a failed one at that."

She took the sketchbook from him and studied it intently. Finally, she looked up.

"Possibly you should see an ophthalmologist," she said at last.

"It's not *that* bad!" he said harshly.

"It's not bad at all," she said, handing it back to him. "But it's not true."

"Explain."

"You tell me your friend Picasso sometimes puts both eyes on the same side of the nose. Is that the way I appear to you when you look at me?"

"No, of course not."

"Then why are you drawing secondhand Picasso sketches instead of firsthand Dali sketches?"

"You don't understand," said Dali. "Drawing a face that way is a very popular convention."

"And is that what you wish to be?" persisted Jinx. "A very popular conventional artist?"

"No," he admitted.

"Well, then?"

He ripped the sketch into tiny pieces.

"And when I get home, I will do the same with the painting," he promised her.

"You painted people with both eyes on the same side of their heads in that, too?" she asked.

"No, but there are other conventions I subscribed to. What I must do is rid myself of all preconceptions, and create works that do not build on what has gone before, that do not borrow from the current trends, but which become artistic first causes in themselves."

"What is an artistic first cause?" she asked curiously.

"You are aware of cause and effect?"

"No."

"But you must be!" insisted Dali. "For every cause, there is an effect."

"Not in my world," said Jinx.

"But there is in mine," he said. "Each effect in turn becomes a cause for the next effect, for whatever follows. This indeed is how Saint Thomas Aquinas proved the existence of God. For every effect, there is a cause, and when we come to the First Cause, that which existed before anything else, we call it God."

"Are you equating what you want to paint with God, then?" asked Jinx curiously.

Dali shook his head impatiently. "Of course not. I am simply saying that I do not want my paintings to be derivative, to be the effect of other artists' causes."

"Yes, I suppose that makes sense."

"Oh, it makes perfect sense," said Dali bitterly. "The trick is *how* to accomplish it."

"That's easy enough," said Jinx.

"All right, my young genius. Suppose you tell me how to do it."

"That would be cheating."

"What are you talking about?" he demanded irritably.

"If I told you, then you'd never be sure it was your own idea—and in fact you'd be right," said Jinx. "Sooner or later you'd convince yourself it was just the whim of a young girl, and you'd abandon it. You'll be much happier if you come up with it yourself."

"When?" he growled. "When I am eighty and half blind?"

"Oh, you'll figure it out sooner than that," she assured him.

"How comforting," he said sardonically.

"It's like the next-to-last chapter in a mystery novel," she said.

"What do you know of mystery novels?"

"I read one in your house while you were sleeping," she replied.

"Fine. How is it like a mystery novel?"

"You already know everything you have to know. Now you just have to put it together."

He was still pondering that when he went to bed a few hours later.

CHAPTER 7

An Angry Figment

"Maybe we should go back through the closet," suggested Dali the next evening.

"Why?" asked Jinx.

"Don't you miss your world?"

"Come on, Salvador," said Jinx. "You don't care whether I miss my world or not. What's your real reason?"

"Has anyone told you that you are an annoying little girl?" asked Dali irritably.

"I thought I was a young lady."

"Only when you are not annoying me."

"*I* am not annoying you," said Jinx. "*You* are."

"So now you not only aspire to be a painter, but to take Sigmund Freud's place and tell me what I am to think?"

"I would never tell you what to think, Salvador," she replied. "I would only tell you to be true to your thoughts."

Dali sighed. "I am surrounded by the mundane and the boring. Why should I expect anything but platitudes from a girl who is barely in her teens?"

"Do you find me mundane and boring?" she asked.

"No," he admitted. "You are perhaps the one thing in my life, besides Gala, that does not bore me." He stared at her. "But you torment me, young Jinx. You know what I need to know, and yet you will not tell me."

"It is too pleasant an evening to argue," she said. "The last rays of the sun will soon be gone, the moon is rising, and there's finally a gentle breeze. Shall we take a walk?"

"Through the park."

She smiled. "Are you afraid someone will see us?"

"I love the motion of moonlight on water," he answered noncommittally.

He walked to the door and opened it for her. She went out, then waited for him.

A pudgy woman was the only other person in the park, walking rapidly along a stone path, and Dali made sure they stayed far enough away that she couldn't see them clearly.

"Why are you avoiding her?" asked Jinx.

"She is a fat cow," said Dali.

"She is not responsible for how she looks."

"We are *all* responsible for how we look," Dali corrected her. "And she is a most unpleasant woman, an obese spinster who pokes her nose into everybody's business. If she could see you clearly, within an hour everyone I know would think you were my new mistress." He glared at the woman. "The fat cow," he repeated.

"How would you paint her?" asked Jinx.

"As she looks," he said. "Gross, ugly, with that mole the size of a thimble on her chin." Suddenly a smile. "Well, on *one* of her chins, anyway."

"That's interesting," remarked Jinx.

"Why? How would you paint her?"

"Exactly the way you just described her," answered Jinx.

"Then why is it interesting that I should do the same?" he asked.

"Because I see her as a woman, and you see her as a cow," said Jinx.

"Then you would have me paint her as a cow?" asked Dali, frowning.

"*I* wouldn't have you paint her any way," she replied. "It's how *you* would paint her."

"A cow," mused Dali. Then, "No, not a cow. That would be ludicrous. But a woman with definite bovine features...*Interesting*." A pause. "I wonder what Freud would say?"

"What difference does it make?" asked Jinx. "He's no artist."

"There you are wrong, young lady," said Dali. "He is as much an artist of the mind as I am of the brush and canvas."

"But the two are different disciplines."

"At their highest level there comes a point at which they merge," said Dali with absolute certainty.

She looked at him curiously.

"I have been giving some thought to all the things you have said to me," he continued. "If I don't see two eyes on the same side of the nose, if I don't see a man or a woman with blue skin, then it is dishonest to paint it. It is not dishonest for Picasso. His paintings are done with such skill and such certainty that it is clear that *is* what he sees. But I don't, and I can't waste my time copying what Freud would find on the inside of Picasso's head if he were ever to examine it. I must paint what *I* see in my head."

"It makes sense to me," said Jinx noncommittally.

"It made sense to me, too—but everything I see is so, well, mundane," said Dali. He kicked at some dirt, lost in thought. Finally he looked up. "But filtered through *my* mind, even the mundane can become wondrous and unique," he said. "Like a bovine woman. Like a boring landscape that my imagination can turn into something"—he searched for a word—"*Daliesque*."

"I think maybe you're on to something, Salvador," said Jinx.

"You *know* I am," said Dali. "You pointed the way to me. When I see something unique, like your world beyond the closet, I will paint it naturalistically, with photographic accuracy. But when I find something dull and ordinary in my own world, rather than reproduce it as it is, or ignore it totally, I will filter it through my mind and paint what I think it *should* be, what it *would* be if it were on *your* side of the door."

Suddenly, he laughed in amusement.

"What is it?" asked Jinx.

"Freud would say I was exorcising my demons, but in fact I shall be capitalizing on them. Everyone has dreams and nightmares, me more than most. Freud made his reputation by expunging them from his subjects, but I will cherish mine, for they will bring me worldwide fame. Who else would be so bold and so innovative as to share his most secret longings, lusts, and fears with the viewing public?"

"So you will paint what you see?"

"No, young Jinx," he said happily. "Or, rather, yes, I will paint what I see—but more to the point, I will paint what no one else sees, what no one else will ever see!"

"Except me," she reminded him.

"Except you what?" he asked, confused.

"You will paint what no one sees except you and me."

"It would be nice if you saw it," he said with a shrug. "It would be nice if you were here, but…"

"But what?"

"I have concluded that you don't exist," said Dali with a confident smile.

"What are you talking about?"

"It's all very Freudian," he said. "I invented you, because I could not approach the conclusion directly. I needed you to point me in the right direction. I don't know why, because it now seems so simple. But I was stymied, mired in mediocrity. Then I spent an afternoon with Freud, I read his books and monographs—and suddenly here you were, an impossible girl from an impossible world, who was created by my subconscious for one reason and one reason only: to point me in the right direction as an artist. I don't know why I couldn't see it myself, but the mind is a strange instrument, and mine required you."

"So that is your conclusion?" replied Jinx. "That I am a figment of your imagination?"

"Absolutely."

"I am going back through the door to my world now, Salvador," she said. "But you owe me painting lessons, and I will be back for them."

"You are never coming back," he said with a dismissive wave of the hand. "You have served my subconscious mind's purpose, and now you will return there."

"I have one question for you before I go back into your brain, Salvador," said Jinx.

"What is it?"

"Could a figment of your imagination do this?"

She kicked him as hard as she could in his left shin.

He howled in anguish and fell over, his hands clutching his leg as she walked back to his house in solitary splendor.

Seven hours later his shin still hurt, it had turned an ugly share of purple, and he was forced to the rueful conclusion that whatever had kicked him, it wasn't an imaginary girl.

CHAPTER 8

New Perspectives

There was a knocking at the door, and Dali raced to open it, hoping it was Jinx, fearful it was Gala with blood in her eye. It turned out to be Ramon the iceman.

"Good morning, Señor Dali," he said, bent under the weight of the ice block he carried on his back.

"Good morning," said Dali, escorting the iceman into the kitchen, where he gently lowered the block of ice to the table, then opened the icebox and began positioning it inside the ice compartment.

"It's a very nice day," said Ramon. "They had predicted rain, but the sun is out, and the weather is pleasant and mild." He looked at the items in the icebox. "You are keeping more fruit and meat than usual."

"I expect guests," said Dali.

"I'll stop by again tomorrow and see if you need more ice," said Ramon. "By the way, have you heard the news?"

"What news are you referring to?"

"I heard on the radio at Gregorio's taverna that no less than six American businessmen committed suicide this month."

"The Depression," said Dali knowingly.

"They should have been here," said Ramon. "We've been depressed for so long that they'd have developed an immunity to it."

He laughed at his own joke and walked to the front door, then stopped.

"What is it?" asked Dali.

"I thought I heard a noise from *there*," he said, pointing in the direction of Dali's studio and bedroom.

"You must be mistaken," said Dali uncomfortably.

"Could be mice," continued Ramon. "Your fruit is quite ripe. You might check your closets. Mice love to hide in them."

"I'll check as soon as you're gone," said Dali.

"I could help you, Señor Dali."

"No," said Dali. "That won't be necessary. I wouldn't want to delay you."

"It's no trouble. I'd be happy to help a famous painter like you."

"I appreciate the offer, but I won't have someone else's food spoil because of your good intentions."

"You're sure?"

Dali nodded, and Ramon finally left.

The painter walked into what he thought of as "Jinx's closet," faced it, and raised his voice. "You can come out now, Jinx."

The door opened, and the redheaded girl approached him.

"Welcome back."

"I told you I would be here for my lesson."

"I half thought…" he began.

"Would you like more proof that I'm real?" she asked with a smile.

"No," he said promptly, his hand moving instinctively toward his shin. "No, that will not be necessary."

"Good," she said. "My toes are still sore from where I kicked you."

"You could have just slapped me, you know."

She shook her head. "It wouldn't have left a bruise," she explained, "and by now you'd have convinced yourself it was all your imagination."

"Probably," he admitted.

"You have a remarkable imagination, Salvador," continued Jinx seriously, wandering over to look at his latest canvas. "You should make it serve you, rather than hindering you."

"I'm all through doubting your existence," said Dali. "But I'm also through with guessing games. Let's proceed with your lesson. If you want to tell me something about myself or my painting, tell me. If not, don't. But no more hints."

"All right, Salvador," she agreed.

"Good," he replied, getting to his feet. "Now, sit," he said, gesturing to his stool.

She sat down. He then covered the canvas that he'd been working on with a large sheet of blank paper and handed her a piece of chalk.

"We will begin," he announced, "with perspective."

"Why?"

"Because every artist experiences reality differently than his peers, and you can alter reality more with perspective than with anything else."

"Explain, please," said Jinx.

"Let me give you an example," replied Dali. "The other night I was awakened by the buzzing of a bee as it flew around a pomegranate. And during those last few seconds of sleep, I dreamed that I was fishing and had hooked a small fish—but as I pulled on my line, the fish opened its mouth and out sprang a full-sized tiger which had been living inside the fish, and it turned out that it was the tiger, rather than the fish, that had really taken my bait."

"It sounds very strange."

"It was—and very frightening," said Dali. "And quite impossible, wouldn't you say?"

"Yes."

"I agree," he said. "Now draw it."

"I can't."

"Why not?"

"How can you show a large tiger emerging from a small fish?" replied Jinx.

"I thought you'd never ask," said Dali with a smile. "You do it with perspective. Here, I will show you."

He took the chalk from her, began sketching furiously, and stood back a moment later.

"Amazing!" said Jinx.

"Perspective," said Dali with a shrug, as if to say: *It's so simple, a child can do it.* "That is what I like about the world behind the closet. Its creator, assuming it has one, uses perspective exactly as I have done here."

"I still must master perspective, and mixing paints, and even such simple things as preparing a canvas," said Jinx. "But you are beyond all that."

"Yes, I am," said Dali, watching her curiously. "I assume you have a point to make?"

"There isn't much meaning in a tiger jumping out of a fish's mouth," she said. "So while I must learn almost everything, what *you* must learn is where to find meaning and how to incorporate it in your painting. For example, drawing the fat cow as a fat cow would be meaningful to you, and now to me, but would it mean anything to anyone who didn't know her, or hadn't heard what you called her?"

"Is it important that it mean anything to anyone but the artist?" retorted Dali, clearly unconvinced.

"If you want an audience, of course it is," she said. "You are a painter. Why did you make that movie?"

"*Un Chien Andalou*?" he said.

"Yes."

"I'm surprised you are aware of it."

"I have studied your life and your work during the time I've been here.

You made a movie. It shocked audiences everywhere. I've never seen it, but I gather at one point someone's eyeball gets slit open with a razor."

"*That* woke them up," said Dali with a chortle.

"It's not funny to do that to someone's eye."

"You don't think we *really* cut a man's eye open, do you?" asked Dali. "It was like…like painting old Señora Mendez as a fat cow. She's not really a cow, and no one sacrificed an eye to make the movie."

"Then why did you do it?"

"To shock the audience, of course," said Dali. "To remind them they're alive, to make them emotional participants rather than mere observers."

She pulled out her sketchbook, and showed him drawings of the park, his own furniture, a dog sleeping on the lawn, and a bird nesting in a nearby tree.

"These aren't as good as yours, of course," she said. "But even if I had your skills, I didn't create these to shock anyone, but to please them."

"Not so, young Jinx," said Dali.

"But look at them. They're not very good, I admit, but they're naturalistic. This is the way the subjects appeared to me."

"And where do you intend to show them?" he asked. "In your world or mine?"

"In mine, of course. I live there; I am just a temporary visitor here."

"Will these be uncontroversial, pastoral pictures in your world?" asked Dali.

"No, probably not," she admitted. "But the artist's purpose is not to shock, but to please. Regardless of the effect, they were drawn—or when I get better they *will* be drawn—for an audience." She walked over to a bookcase and withdrew a volume. "The author of this book wanted it to be read by others. If not, he could simply recite stories to himself in the shower and save all that wear and tear on his fingers and his typewriter. By the same token, you paint because you want to share your vision with the rest of the world. Admittedly, it has to be a unique vision to be of any lasting worth, but if it is such that only you can understand it, why should anyone care to look at it?"

"People have always been fascinated by the bizarre," answered Dali. "They would look at the fat cow simply because they have never seen a cow, fat or otherwise, walking erect, wearing a dress, bursting out of a girdle, and carrying a purse."

"That is true," agreed Jinx. "Paint anything bizarre and they will look, just as they watched an eye being cut open. Draw a man with two heads or a nude woman with three breasts, or a baby that is bigger than yourself, and they will look. But such paintings would just be curiosity pieces, just like *Un Chien Andalou*, which is already forgotten by almost everyone. Such paintings would not touch or move your audience, because they would be tricks. They would have nothing of *you* in them."

"But I *am* bizarre," said Dali.

"You pretend to be."

"How could I not be?" he insisted. "I am a replacement for my dead brother. My father killed my mother, and I have said so publicly. I had my first art exhibit when I was fifteen, while all the other boys my age were busy playing soccer. Everything about me is strange and bizarre."

"Then you must paint bizarre things that have meaning to your audience."

Dali couldn't quite repress a smile. "Have you been talking to Freud?"

"Why?" she asked. "Do I sound like him?"

"Very much."

"I've never met him," Jinx assured him. "But you talk about him incessantly."

"He has had a profound effect on my thinking," replied Dali. "He's taught me that the visions I see, the images that come to me, have meaning if I can just comprehend them. He has encouraged me to explore all the hidden corners of my mind—my dreams, my fears, my lusts, my longings, my nightmares—and since they are all essential parts of myself, he tells me that I should find ways to use them in my art. And you, young Jinx, have told me much the same."

"Then perhaps there's something to it," she said.

"I know there is," said Dali. "But what?"

"I'm sure Dr. Freud would say that is for you to decide."

"It is very confusing," he admitted. "The other day we were discussing limp watches. The day I met you I saw a red elephant walking on twenty-foot-tall stiltlike legs. I know I am to find meaning in the images that I see and that I imagine—but what meaning is there in such a beast, or a burning giraffe, or a limp watch?"

"Do you know what I think?" said Jinx.

"What?"

"When you know the answer to that, you'll be ready to paint them and stun the world."

CHAPTER 9

The Camembert of Time

"Good afternoon, Salvador."

"Good afternoon, young lady," said Dali, looking up from the newspaper he had been reading. "Where have you been these last two days?"

"I have a home, you know."

"I don't really know it," answered Dali. "I have a feeling I might still be imagining you." Suddenly, he tensed. "No! Don't kick me again!"

She laughed. "All right, you're safe. For the moment." She stared at him. "You didn't wash your face after lunch."

"Oh?"

"You've got something on your upper lip."

"*That*," he explained with some dignity, "is the beginning of my mustache."

"Why are you growing a mustache?" she asked.

"To make myself unique, as we discussed."

"Maybe it has escaped your attention," said Jinx, obviously unimpressed, "but millions of men have mustaches."

"Not like mine will be," answered Dali confidently. "It may take me a

year, it may take me five years, but when I am done, it will be the most rec-
ognizable mustache in the entire world. The ends of it will be four inches
long, and I will wax them and train them to stand straight up."

"It'll be distinctive, that's for sure," said Jinx. "What will Gala say when
she sees it?"

"What do I care?" Dali shot back. "It is *my* mustache." He paused
uncomfortably. "Besides, I will make sure she sees it from a distance first."

"Or perhaps in a crowd?" suggested Jinx.

"That would not deter her," he replied grimly.

"Deter her from what?"

"Don't ask."

"You make me very afraid of her," said Jinx.

"Welcome to the club," he said wryly.

"Then why do you keep seeing her?"

"Because while I may occasionally fear for my life in her presence, the
fact remains that I love her more than life itself," answered Dali.

"I hope it doesn't come to a choice," said Jinx.

"Between what?" he asked, confused.

"Between Gala and life itself."

"She only wants what is best for me," said Dali defensively. "Just as
you do."

"Then why are you not afraid of me?" asked Jinx.

"Let us change the subject."

"Whatever you wish."

"I wish to discuss some ideas with you," said Dali.

"I am flattered," said Jinx. "What shall we discuss?"

"Many things," answered Dali. "It is finally time to systematize con-
fusion and thus to help discredit completely the world of reality."

"You have been thinking about what I said," replied Jinx happily.

"I have. It is time for a break with my past. When I created the film, *Un
Chien Andalou*, the Surrealists accepted me as one of their own—but I am

not like them, any more than I am like Picasso, or for that matter Michelangelo. I am Dali, who must be like no one else." He got to his feet. "I grow weary of *my* world. It is time to visit yours once more."

"Why?"

"I have an idea of what I want to paint, but I feel I need to see it once more." He paused. "Will you be my guide?"

She nodded her assent. "Of course. Otherwise, you might get lost and never find your way back."

"You never get lost on *my* side of the door," he noted almost enviously.

"That's because I have a logical mind," answered Jinx. "You have a brilliant mind, but logic is not one of its virtues."

She held out her hand and led him to the closet, then through the door at the back of it, and a moment later he was once again in Jinx's world, where cause followed effect, up was down, and black was white.

"Hi there, Jinx," said a voice. "I see you've brought a friend."

Dali turned and found himself facing a giraffe.

"Was that *you*?" he asked.

"Most assuredly," said the giraffe.

"But giraffes can't make any sound at all," said Dali. "Everyone knows that."

"Silliest thing I ever heard," replied the giraffe. "Or do you think I'm not making any sounds?"

"I apologize," said Dali. "Clearly I was the victim of false doctrine." He stared at the creature. "I think I saw you the last time I was here."

"It's possible. I live here."

"But you were on fire then."

The giraffe shrugged. "It was a hot day."

"That's not a valid reason," protested Dali. "After all, you aren't covered with snow today."

"I don't like snow."

"Are you saying you like being on fire?"

"You've been standing here talking to me," replied the giraffe. "Did I say that?"

"No, but…"

"Jinx, maybe you should knead your friend's brain the way you might knead a loaf of bread. It's much too rigid."

"Then tell me what you represent when you're on fire," said Dali.

"What I represent?" repeated the giraffe. "You make it sound like I've got a constituency that votes for me because I catch on fire."

"That's not what I meant," protested Dali.

"A giraffe's life is too busy to worry about what you meant."

And with that, the giraffe ran off.

"He's right, you know," said Dali after a moment's thought.

"About what?"

"I *am* too rigid. Surrealism is just another discipline, and if one can call it a discipline, then it is already suffering from hardening of the arteries. This brief interlude with the giraffe reminds me that I have come here to free myself of all my preconceptions. I would like it to be said someday that the only difference between Dali and a madman is that Dali is not quite mad."

He began walking through the strange and ever-changing landscape, peering intently into the distance.

"What are you looking for?" asked Jinx at last.

"Something I saw the last time I was here."

"Things change," responded Jinx. "My world is much like yours in that respect. Perhaps if you'll tell me what you're looking for…"

"Those limp clocks."

"They're not here."

"You're sure?"

"You saw them days ago. They weren't keeping time fast enough to make it all the way up to today." She paused. "They'll probably be here next week—but of course, you'll be a week ahead of them."

"That is wonderful!" exclaimed Dali.

"That you can't see what you came here to see?" she asked, confused.

"That you gave me a totally nonsensical answer that makes absolute sense to me," he said.

"I don't understand."

"All the better," said Dali. "All right, we can go back to my side of the door."

"You're sure?"

"I'm sure. If I stayed here, I'd be the most realistic painter of this world. I'd rather be the least realistic of my own—and with the very same paintings."

"Why did you want to see the clocks?" she asked as they began walking through the dreamlike, angular landscape.

"Just to study them."

"What about them interests you?"

"I don't like Time," said Dali. "It robs us of our youth and beauty. Eventually, it burdens us with so many years that we can barely carry them on our backs. The load becomes so heavy that we walk stooped over or with a cane, and eventually we cannot bear the weight of our years any longer. As far as I am concerned, Time is a villain."

"An interesting way of looking at it," Jinx admitted.

"I want to create a painting in which Time loses all meaning, where the rigid ticking of seconds and hours and years becomes as soft as, I don't know, as overripe cheese." He paused, considering the concept. "Yes, I think that the limp watches will represent the camembert of Time."

"Then that's *it*?" asked Jinx, obviously disappointed. "You're going to create a painting that contains nothing but limp watches?"

"No," answered Dali. "But they are a start, a theme. Everything else will support that theme, strengthen it, add to it."

"And what will this 'everything else' be?" asked Jinx, as the closet door suddenly appeared in the middle of a dark purple sand dune a quarter mile away.

"That is what we have to talk about, isn't it?" answered Dali, heading toward the door.

CHAPTER 10

The Greatest Villain

"You see?" asked Dali, briefly sketching the limp watches. "I cannot do an entire painting of just the watches. If it is to have any meaning, I must show…*what*?" He looked at the sketch. "It must be staring me in the face, but I do not see it. Yet I have the methodology now that I've read and spoken to Freud."

"You do?"

He nodded absently, still studying the sketch. "I call it my paranoiac-critical method, which is really a tip of the hat to my friend Sigmund, who gave me the word 'paranoiac'. Your world gave me the rest."

"What exactly do you think my world gave you that you didn't have before?" asked Jinx.

"You'll get mad if I tell you."

"Perhaps—but unlike Gala, I won't hit you."

"Freud has pointed out in his work that hallucinations are very much like dreams: they are the mind's way of giving some shape or form to secret fears and longings. Clearly I have learned to induce psychotic hallucinations myself, for what else could your world behind the closet possibly be?"

"It is my home," she said. "And if I have to kick you again to prove that I am real, I will."

"I told you that my answer would make you mad," said Dali with a knowing smile.

"Would you like proof that my world exists?" asked Jinx.

"Why not?" he replied, then hastily added: "I do not consider inflicting physical pain an acceptable proof."

"Fine," she said promptly. "Call your friend Lorca, the writer, and invite him over. Or better still, this Picasso you keep talking about. Don't tell them what they're about to see, so when they enter my world you can't claim the observations were due to the power of suggestion."

"*No!*" he said so harshly that it startled her. She stared at him expectantly but said nothing. "If it is not real, they will lock me away for my own good."

"No, they won't," replied Jinx. "They already think you're somewhere between eccentric and half-mad, and they leave you alone. What is the *real* reason?"

"I won't share it with another artist!" he shouted.

"Lorca isn't a painter, he's a writer."

"He's a *literary* artist."

"Well, at least you're honest. But just as people have different perceptions of your world, I think your friends would see things that you do not see, and miss things that are very plain to you."

"But you don't *know* it, do you?" he persisted.

"No, Salvador, I don't know it. Both our worlds change and evolve, but mine does so a lot faster. Even *I* am confused by it from time to time."

"As I am confused by mine," he said. Suddenly, he smiled. "I think that's it."

"That is what?"

"That is part of the answer I have been seeking for my painting."

"I don't understand," said Jinx.

"We remember the way our worlds were the last time we experienced them," he said. "But they change, however subtly, with the passage of time. That's why the world can be so confusing. Because I remember it as it was, but as I said, Time is a villain. It deludes us, and I will show that with the limp watches."

"I'm not following you."

"*Who* is Time deluding? *Who* remembers things as they were, and has difficulty adjusting to things as they are?"

"Everyone."

"But *everyone* isn't creating the painting," he pointed out. "*I* am."

"Then you are going to be the subject of your own painting?" she asked.

He shook his head impatiently. "I will be *in* the painting, but the subject is Time, and the way it fools memory—and just as Time will be represented by watches that are as soft as overripe cheese, watches that are losing their structural integrity, that is the way I myself must be represented."

"I don't understand," said Jinx, frowning. "Why must you also be soft?"

"More than soft," answered Dali. "I must be almost shapeless."

"Still, why?"

"If I painted myself as I am, I would be saying that Time has no effect on me, that no matter how inaccurate my memories become with the passage of Time, I am exactly the same man I would be if Time did not pass at all."

He leaned forward and began sketching a grotesquely misshapen body. Finally, he finished and leaned back.

"What do you think?" he asked Jinx.

"I don't like it," she said. "No one will ever know it's a human, let alone that it's you."

"They don't have to know it's me, as long as *I* know it," he said. "But I agree. I can't put in the details I want if I use my entire body. I think I'll just use a hugely distorted head."

He sketched again, then stopped and stared at what he'd done.

"It doesn't look like a head," said Jinx.

"It has eyelashes and a nose," noted Dali. "What else could it possibly be?"

"In a world with limp clocks? It could be anything."

"Then I will provide it with another facial feature, perhaps two," said Dali. "But first I will have to consider what features to use."

"And where will the watches be?" asked Jinx.

"Good question," he said. "I have been thinking about it, and I believe I have the answer."

"What is it?"

He pointed to a corner of the studio. "Stand over there."

She did as he asked.

"Now count to three."

"One. Two. Three."

"Very good," he said. "Now go stand by the door to the kitchen."

She did so.

"Count again."

"One. Two. Three."

"Well, there you have it," said Dali, nodding his head in satisfaction.

"There I have *what*?" asked Jinx, puzzled.

"Don't you see?" said Dali. "Time doesn't exist just in the corner, or just by the door, or here at the easel. It's *everywhere* at once."

"I knew that."

"Sometimes the things we know are the least obvious to us," said Dali. "Since Time is everywhere at once, what I must do is create a landscape, to show that Time is not merely a villain in my studio, or whatever museum or private home in which the painting eventually hangs. To show the universality of the theme, I must show a large landscape."

"You could show the watches in outer space, or on Mars," suggested Jinx.

"An intriguing suggestion," he said, suddenly interested. Then he shook his head. "No, I do not know for a fact that Time is a villain on Mars. Probably it is, but I have never been to Mars or outer space, so I can't be sure. I will paint the watches on Earth—but in a landscape that cannot be identified as Spain or anywhere else. That will show that it is true everywhere." He paused to consider the painting further, then continued: "I think the landscape must be bleak beyond imagining, to show the detritus of Time's march through the world. Perhaps I will even hang one of the watches on the leafless limb of a dead tree, to emphasize that fact." He paused. "Yes, that will work. And I will use no undiluted primary colors, which will further lend to the effect." He frowned briefly. "But I still need something else, something to hold the attention."

"Don't you think limp watches and a barely human face will hold the attention?" asked Jinx.

"They will *capture* the attention. But I must add something more, something small, to *hold* the attention. Something that is not obvious at first, but that they will see when they study the painting, which will force them to study it further." He sighed deeply. "I am still not considering all the facets of this painting. Time affects more than the memory. Eventually, it will kill you and me and every living thing. Even rocks will decay in the fullness of time. Time is not only a villain, but a murderer. I must make that clear."

"How much bleaker can you make it?" asked Jinx curiously.

"In that direction lies disaster," replied Dali. "That would make the painting so bleak, so lifeless, that no one would look at it for more than a few seconds before they were overcome by hopelessness and depression. No, the answer lies elsewhere." He turned to her. "And of course you know what it is."

"Why should you say that?"

"Because, my precocious young lady, every other aspect of the painting is due to your input, so surely you know what else is needed to make it perfect."

"I never told you to paint limp watches and a misshapen face," said Jinx. "They're your own ideas."

"But it was you who convinced me to search for unique ideas," answered Dali. "Who else in all the world would paint a limp watch? Who else would paint an elephant on stiltlike legs, which I shall certainly do one of these days. No, Jinx, you may not have said 'Paint this!' or 'Draw that!', but you were the one who convinced me to look for things that only I can see and paint. So," he concluded, "what is the answer? What more must I put into the painting?"

"I really don't know," said Jinx.

"And if you did, you wouldn't tell me anyway, would you?" asked Dali.

"Probably not," she admitted. "But I really and truly don't know."

"Then I must study it further and come up with the solution myself."

He turned back to the sketch and sat motionless in front of it for the better part of an hour.

"Bah!" he said. "I need air. I am going out for a walk."

"I'll come with you."

"Well," he said, putting on a satin cape and grabbing a silver-headed cane, "let's go, then."

"It's quite warm out," she said. "You don't need the cape."

"I don't wear it for *me*," he said disdainfully. "I wear it for *them*."

"Them?"

"The same people I use the cane for, the same people I will cultivate the mustache for. In brief, everyone but me."

"And me," added Jinx.

"And you," he agreed, opening the door for her.

CHAPTER 11

The Finishing Touch

They had walked through the empty streets for perhaps an hour. Twice they passed men Dali knew. Both times, the men grunted a greeting but never mentioned Jinx. As they continued their stroll, Dali became silent and seemingly morose, lost in his thoughts about the painting. Jinx hummed a bouncy tune, stopped to pet a stray dog, sketched a pigeon that perched on a window ledge.

"Why are you so happy?" asked Dali at last.

"Why shouldn't I be?" she replied. "It's a beautiful day, the sun is out, and I am finally getting used to this world, to the patterns of its streets and buildings, to the way every single person bears such a striking resemblance to every other person. You don't always find that in my world."

"I know," he said. "Perhaps that is why I prefer painting your world to my own."

"Have you come up with any ideas yet?"

"Either sixty-three or sixty-four, I lost count." He grimaced. "Each was worse than the last."

"Well, cheer up. It will come to you."

"I wish I had your confidence."

They walked another block, and suddenly she stopped humming.

"Oh, that's so sad!" she said.

"What is?" asked Dali distractedly.

She pointed to a small cat that lay dead in the street some forty yards ahead of them. "I think a car must have killed the poor thing. Probably it happened last night and the driver never saw it."

"Unless it happened today, and the driver hated cats," shot back Dali, whose inability to solve his problem was making him argumentative.

"No," said Jinx with certainty as they walked closer to the cat. "It was killed last night."

"Let me guess," said Dali sarcastically. "You've read another mystery novel and you're practicing your detection."

She shook her head. "It's just common sense." She pointed to the cat. "It's covered by ants and flies. If it had just been killed, that many insects wouldn't have discovered it yet."

Dali stopped and stared at the cat for a long moment. Then he uttered a surprised laugh and thrust a fist triumphantly above his head.

"What a blessing you turned out to be!" he said happily.

"I don't understand."

"I need to suggest death and decay," he said, "but if I make the painting any bleaker, people will turn away from it, you've convinced me of that. *But,*" he added, "what if I have insects crawling across the faces of the watches? People are fascinated by them because they are as different from us as any living things can be. They are disgusted by them, too, because sooner or later everyone has seen insects doing exactly what they are doing to the remains of that cat. But if there is no life in the painting, that will mean Time has won, and what is left are the insects. They will have nothing to eat, so they will be crawling across the faces of the watches, just as they have crawled across the face of the world for hundreds of millions of years. Things come and things go, but insects remain, the one constant among

Nature's creations."

"I think it'll look creepy," offered Jinx.

"Yes, it will," agreed Dali. "But that will fascinate the viewer, rather than so depress him that he walks away."

"So that's the answer—insects?" asked Jinx dubiously. "You're going to use dull colors to paint a bleak, barren landscape, a misshapen face, some limp watches, and some insects. And that's *it*?"

"It sounds terrible, doesn't it?" replied Dali with a smile. He tapped his temple with a forefinger. "But when I see it in here, I know that it will be the greatest thing I have ever painted, maybe the greatest I ever *will* paint."

"You're sure?"

"I'm sure. And I owe it all to you and Freud."

"Before you go thanking anyone, perhaps you should paint it first and see if you're still pleased with it," suggested Jinx.

"The actual painting is the easy part," said Dali. "Trust me on this. This work will become the talk of the art world. It will secure my future as an artist."

"Just watches and insects and a face?"

"And a vision," he added. "*My* vision."

"What will you call it?"

"I expect you to vanish when I finish it—don't kick me! I haven't figured out how an imaginary girl manages to do that yet—but I shall be eternally grateful to you, and I will never forget you. And since the painting is about Time anyway, I will combine the two notions and call it *The Persistence of Memory*."

"I like it," she said. "I wonder if anyone else will."

She had her answer a month later.

CHAPTER 12

The Persistence of Gala

The painting was an instant sensation. Critics of every type, no matter what their tastes, acknowledged it as a work of genius. Not all of them agreed on its meaning, and Dali, making the most of it, gave each a different interpretation when asked. It made no difference; he had moved from being a very good painter to being an acknowledged master with a single painting.

Publicly, Dali was self-assured. Of course he knew audiences would love his painting. No, he never doubted its effect. Yes, he knew from the first instant what he was going to put in the painting and what it meant.

Privately, he was alternately surprised and bitter—surprised that a single painting had made his name known throughout the world, even among people who had no interest in art; and bitter, because he was convinced that he'd been producing paintings of almost the same quality for years and had been ignored by the world beyond the art colony.

"Well," he concluded one evening when he and Jinx were taking a walk along the seashore, "at least one thing will come of the painting, other than notoriety. I will be rich enough and famous enough for Gala to finally leave her husband and marry me."

"You really want that?" asked Jinx, who had a difficult time under-standing his relationship with this woman she had never seen.

"I love her more than life itself," said Dali. "If I could, I would spend the rest of my life covering her hands and feet with kisses. I would face the brave bulls in the arena for her. I would don the uniform of the soldier and languish in the trenches for her."

"You'd do all that for her?" asked Jinx.

"Absolutely," Dali assured her. "She is the heart of my heart and soul of my soul." He paused uncomfortably. "I just wish I wasn't so frightened of her."

"She's not going to harm the meal ticket that produced *The Persistence of Memory*," said Jinx.

"She will be after me night and day to produce an even greater painting, and then one that is greater still."

"Perhaps she just wants the best for you," said Jinx. "Or for her."

"Her only flaw is that she is just a bit too possessive," said Dali. "She does not like me to spend time with any of my friends, and she seems as jealous of men as of women, though of course she has no reason to be."

"All right, she's possessive," said Jinx. "We all have our faults. That's not a terrible one."

"No, of course not," said Dali. "There are worse things than being possessive. And domineering. And jealous. And occasionally violent."

"She must have some good qualities," said Jinx, who had yet to hear Dali mention any.

"She loves me," he replied. "What better quality could one want?" He sighed. "Of course, she doesn't love me enough to marry me until I have more money than her current husband—but an exquisite creature like that *needs* to have gifts and money showered upon her."

"I thought you were going to put her face in every painting you did?"

"Her face or her body," he acknowledged. "Well, perhaps not every one. She won't mind if she is not in each painting. What will enrage her is if I put someone else in a painting." He looked at her. "Like you, for instance."

"Well, then you shouldn't paint me."

"That's what we have to talk about."

"Painting me?" she asked, surprised.

"No. But what to paint next. I think it's time I visited the world behind the closet again."

"I don't think so."

"*What?*" demanded Dali in panicky tones.

"You have been there twice. If you go back there every time you want to create another painting, you will never paint your own world."

"My own world is incredibly dull. I have made my reputation for all time by painting *your* world."

"They are the same, you know."

"Ridiculous!" snapped Dali. "I have been to your world. It is nothing like mine."

"You yourself explained it the first day you taught me to paint," answered Jinx. "The difference is perspective. I have a home and a family, I have friends and pets, we have farms and cities, trees and flowers. You have the same things. Each world simply imposes a different perspective on its inhabitants."

"I shall have to think about that," said Dali. "It is a very interesting observation."

Jinx glanced out the window. "You have something more immediate to think about, Salvador."

"What is that?"

"Based on the drawings of her you have shown me, I would say that Gala has come to pay you a visit."

"Omigod!" whispered Dali, ashen-faced. "What am I to do with you?"

"Introduce me as your cousin."

"She knows all my cousins! Quick, go back through the closet!"

"She's at the front door right now. She'll hear me moving through the closet."

"The bathroom—fast!" said Dali desperately, giving her a shove in the right direction, then racing to the front door just as Gala knocked at it.

"Why, Gala!" he said. "What a surprise! I did not know you had returned from Paris."

"All they can talk about in Paris is your painting," she said, turning her head and offering him a cheek to kiss. He chose instead to kiss her hand. She pulled it away with an expression of distaste when he had finished.

"May I offer you some wine?" asked Dali.

"No, thank you," said Gala. "Why are you so breathless and red of face?"

"It is entirely due to the pleasure of seeing you, of course," he answered.

"You seem nervous, Salvador," she said.

"Me?" he asked innocently.

"Have you been seeing another woman while I was gone?"

"Certainly not. I have been painting my masterpiece while you were gone."

She walked to the bedroom and stared at the neatly made bed, then went to the studio, turned to face him, and spoke: "I'll believe you—for now." She glanced at some half-finished canvases. "How many commissions have you gotten since you produced *The Persistence of Memory*?"

"Four."

"For how much?"

"What difference does it make?" responded Dali. "I will never hurt for money again."

"What difference does it make?" repeated Gala. "Are you mad? Overnight you have become the preeminent artist on the continent, the only man mentioned in the same breath as Picasso. You must demand payment equivalent with your status. Now, how much were you offered?"

He named a figure.

"You are worth three times that much," said Gala. "I think I will become your manager as of right now. And the first thing we will do is renegotiate those fees."

"But I have already begun preliminary work on two of the paintings," protested Dali.

"Don't you understand?" replied Gala angrily. "You are Salvador Dali! If these men don't agree to the new fees, then I will sell them on the open market for even more!"

Dali shrugged, feeling overwhelmed as he always did in Gala's presence.

"And now you will take me out to the best restaurant in Madrid," said Gala.

"Are you hungry?" asked Dali.

"Why else would I go to a restaurant?" she said.

To see and be seen, he thought, but he merely shrugged again and said nothing.

"Let me just step into the bathroom and fix my makeup, and we'll leave," announced Gala.

Dali instantly grabbed her arm. She turned to face him, and for an instant he thought she might hit him.

"It's a mess," he said. "I was washing paint off, and it's all over the sink and mirror. I'll clean them later. Come on, let's go and you can put on your face at the restaurant."

Her nose wrinkled. "I don't smell any oil or turpentine," she said. "Perhaps it's not as dirty as you think."

She took a tentative step toward the bathroom, and he retained his hold on her arm.

"I was using water colors as a preliminary medium," he said. "That's why it doesn't smell—but it's filthy. You have such a lovely suit on, I would hate to see it ruined."

The thought of ruining her suit convinced her to listen to him, and they headed for the front door.

As they did, a blue eye watched them through the keyhole of the bathroom door.

Poor man, she thought. *You have many faults and many weaknesses, but you deserve better than this.*

CHAPTER 13

Wedded Blitz

The change occurred almost overnight. Suddenly, every painting Dali produced was eagerly awaited, endlessly analyzed, and sold for sums that had seemed impossible to him only a year earlier. Critics began to see certain themes recurring in his work, and offers came in not only for paintings but speaking engagements and even an autobiography. The editors of two art magazines actually got into a fistfight over the meaning of the limp watches, and a woman Dali had never seen before wrote an article insisting that she had been the model for the misshapen face. (No one believed her except Gala, who was certain that the woman was Dali's secret mistress and screamed at him so loudly and so long that he actually lost the hearing in his left ear for a full day.)

But as Dali's star ascended, Jinx reported that she had problems of her own. She hoped they were the same problems Dali had had as a young man, so that he might be able to tell her how best to cope with them. It seemed that her peers on her side of the door thought she'd gone off the deep end. After all, who had ever heard of a square room or a level floor? Why did all the horses have the same dull manes and tails, and all the dogs the same number of legs? Why did rain and snow come down, when everyone knew they were just as likely to float *up*?

"Are you being true to your inner vision?" asked Dali when she put the question to him during one of her increasingly infrequent visits.

"It's not a matter of an inner vision," answered Jinx. "I paint what I see, and when I am here I see things that make my friends think I am crazy." Her face reflected her concern. "What can I do about it?"

"Revel in it!" said Dali. "Anything that makes you unique is good. Everyone thinks I am crazy; well, everyone except Freud, anyway—and all that has done is enhance the value of my work." Suddenly he smiled. "Correct me if I'm mistaken, but didn't I learn that from *you*?"

"It works for you," answered Jinx, "but I don't *want* to be unique. I am just a girl, and all I want to do is paint the things I see. You are the one who was striving to find things that matched your bizarre mental images, not I. *You* came to *my* world; *I* didn't come to *yours*."

"I was drawn to it," said Dali, feeling defensive without knowing why.

"That doesn't alter the fact that it was you who sought out the unusual and the bizarre, not me," said Jinx. "I merely stumbled upon it when I escorted you back to your side of the door."

"All right," said Dali with a shrug. "If you won't brag about the bizarre visions you capture on canvas, if you won't take full credit for it, then the only alternative is to ignore the critics."

"They're not critics, they're my friends," she said. "I'm just a girl, remember?"

"Now that I come to think of it, that's very curious," said Dali.

"What is?"

Dali walked slowly around her, staring at her intently as he did so.

"Very curious indeed," he repeated. "I hadn't noticed it before, or at least I hadn't paid any attention to it, but you haven't aged a minute since I first met you."

"Time enslaves *your* world, not mine," she answered. "It is much more elastic on my side of the door."

"And there is something else I never noticed until right now," continued Dali. "Except for the hair color, you could be Gala's younger sister. In fact, you could be Gala at age thirteen."

"I hope that's not why you befriended me," said Jinx. "I am my own person."

"No, that's not why I befriended you," said Dali, "though it has become obvious to me that I am drawn to women and girls with Gala's features. It is just an interesting observation." He paused, still studying her face. "I have never asked you before, but based on what you know of her, what is your opinion of Gala?"

"Why do you ask?" she replied suspiciously.

"Because," said Dali, looking more apprehensive than excited, "we have set a date for our marriage."

"I hope the two of you will be very happy together," said Jinx, trying to keep the doubt out of her voice.

"I shall be ecstatically happy," he replied without much assurance.

Funny, she thought. *I never knew you were a masochist. I wonder what your friend Freud would make of it.* Aloud she said, "Then I am ecstatically happy for you."

"It means that you and I will have to be even more discreet in our meetings," he continued.

"If she loves you enough to marry you," replied Jinx, "she should love you enough to believe you when you tell her that we are just friends."

Dali sighed deeply. "You do not know Gala. She is absolute perfection, of course—but she is not always reasonable. Still, I love her desperately and I need her even more. There are so many things I cannot do. I cannot cook, or clean my clothes, or manage my money. She will take over all these functions and free me to paint."

"You are free to paint right now," noted Jinx.

"Ah, but Gala says it is time to grow up."

"Doesn't that mean that it's time to learn to handle money and feed yourself?" she asked innocently.

"You are too young to understand," he said uncomfortably. "Someday you will grow up."

"Someday you may, too," said Jinx.

"I resent that!"

"Then I apologize," she said with obvious insincerity.

"I have but a single fear," said Dali after a moment's silence.

"Only one?" asked Jinx. "I should think you would have many." *All inspired by Gala*, she added silently.

"No, just one," said Dali. "This place is not fitting for a woman of Gala's breeding and quality, and she has explained that it is even less fitting for a man with my current income and prospects. So I think I may be moving after the wedding." He grimaced involuntarily. "That means that I will not be able to visit your world again."

"I wouldn't be too sure of that," said Jinx.

"Oh?"

"Of course, I don't know it for a fact, but I think the doorway will follow you wherever you go."

"What makes you think so?" he asked hopefully.

"I don't know. I just have a feeling that the doorway is *yours* rather than the closet's. I've asked around, and no one remembers seeing the door before you moved into this place, and now everyone sees it plain as day."

Dali closed his eyes, an expression of enormous relief on his face. "I pray that you are right."

"We'll know soon enough," said Jinx. "Now let me see what you have been working on."

CHAPTER 14

Escape

Gala and Dali took up residence in a bigger place, though it was another two years before they were actually married.

In the meantime, she began separating him from his friends, one by one. She was jealous of women, but she was also jealous of men, children, dogs, cats, anything that took Dali's attention away from her.

The one exception was his painting. She knew a good thing when she saw it, and she never interfered with his methods, his subject matter, or anything else concerning his art—except to suggest, as prolific as he was, that he become even more so, that popularity didn't always last and the more paintings he could sell now, the better.

She also encouraged his public eccentricities. She helped wax and train his mustache, and within two years it had become his trademark, as famed throughout the world as his painting was.

She even wrote out some answers for him, after finding out some of the questions that were to be asked in an interview. Examples:

Question: Why do you wear a mustache?

Answer: In order to pass unobserved.

Question: What is surrealism?
Answer: Surrealism is myself.

Question: It has been suggested that your paintings are great
jokes, done at the expense of the critics. Is there any truth to
that?
Answer: It is not necessary for the public to know whether I am
joking or whether I am serious, just as it is not necessary for
me to know it myself.

By the time of their wedding in 1934, Gala had turned him into the
public's favorite celebrity, the probably insane genius of Madrid. Then she
decided that the press was taking up too much of his painting time, as well
as too much of the time he spent with her, and she severely limited its
access to him.

This actually made him even more of a celebrity, the mad recluse who
emerged every month or two with a new painting that the critics could
argue about until the next one appeared.

His new studio, a huge room off the living room, had a small closet to
hold his supplies—and the day they moved in he found a door at the back
of it. He covered it with blank canvases, and since Gala's sole interest was in
his finished work, not in the production of it, she never opened the closet.

Dali rarely saw Jinx after he moved in, but she showed up twice while
Gala was out shopping, once to see what he had painted during the spring
and summer, and once to issue him a warning.

"A warning?" repeated Dali.

"War is coming," she said. "In fact, many wars. It is time for you to
leave the country."

"Leave Spain?" he replied incredulously. "Are you mad? This is my
home."

"Your art has made you a citizen of the world. I really think you should take up residence in a safe part of it—though soon there will be no place that is totally safe."

"What do you know of such things?" he scoffed. "You are just a child, and not even a child of this world."

"You see things no one else can see," said Jinx. "I see things *everyone* except you can see. War is coming, and it is coming to Spain sooner than to most places."

"If you are referring to that failed German artist, that Hitler," said Dali, "then you are mistaken. No one who paints that poorly can present any kind of a threat."

She stared at him for a long moment. "I should not say this to someone who is older than me, and especially to someone who has shown me so many kindnesses—but you are a fool, Salvador. Flee while you still can."

"I know a few people are unhappy with the government," said Dali, "but you are overreacting. This is *Spain*."

"I tried to warn you," she said unhappily. "If you survive, I hope I will see you again, wherever you end up. If not, I have enjoyed our friendship."

"No one's dying and no one's leaving," said Dali. Suddenly, he heard Gala's footsteps approaching the house. "Except you, right now."

"Good-bye, Salvador."

When he had dinner with Gala, he asked her about the current political situation.

"Who has been discussing it with you?" she demanded suspiciously.

"No one," replied Dali. "But I hear things."

"From who?"

"Damn it!" he snapped. "Just tell me about it!"

She glared at him angrily. "The poor and the dispossessed are unhappy. The poor and the dispossessed are *always* unhappy. It is not for you to worry about. You must concentrate on your painting. The government is quite capable of keeping the peasants in their place."

He believed her, and since it would never occur to him to disobey her, he went back to his painting. It was only when they traveled to Catalonia in October, where Dali was to give a lecture on surrealism, that the real world intruded. The lecture was canceled due to violence in the streets, and the Dalis, hoping it would be rescheduled, spent the night at the home of Gala's friend Josep Dalman.

But by morning the Spanish Civil War was raging, with pitched battles taking place in Madrid, Barcelona, and Asturias. At noon, Catalonia declared independence.

Gala knew they couldn't return to their elegant dwelling in Madrid, and she spent most of the day securing a safe-conduct pass and a driver who was willing to risk taking them to the French border.

They were stopped a mile short of the border by rebels who took one look at their expensive clothes and declared that they should be shot on general principles. Dali was too terrified to speak, and Gala was so imperious that she did nothing but enrage the gunmen. It was their driver who took charge of the situation, explained what a safe-conduct pass was to the mostly illiterate rebels, and finally was allowed to cross over into France.

Dali and Gala made their way to Paris by train and bus, where they received news that their driver had been killed by stray machine-gun fire. They spent the night in a hotel, then hunted up an apartment the next day. It took Dali two more days to acquire the supplies he needed, but soon he was painting again—and this time, although it was still surrealistic, it was done with passion and purpose.

One day, after they'd been there for two weeks, Gala went out to Coco Chanel's to have some dresses designed, and Dali, on a hunch, looked in the back of each closet. He had looked the day they moved in, and there had been no door; he looked now, and the result was the same. He decided that he had lost his friend Jinx forever, and was feeling very morose about it, when there was a knock at the door. He opened it and found himself confronting the redheaded girl.

"You!" he exclaimed.

"I am glad to see you finally took my advice," she said, walking past him and entering the apartment. "This is very nice. Not as nice as your house in Madrid, but much nicer than the first place we met."

"How did you get here?" asked Dali.

"The same way as always."

He shook his head. "No you didn't," he said. "There are no doors in the back of any of my closets—and you came in through the front door."

She smiled. "You have a storage closet in the basement."

"We do?" he responded, surprised.

"Yes."

"I didn't even know the building had a basement," he admitted.

"Officially, your storage closet is part of the apartment." She paused. "It's quite empty. The door to my world is in the back of it."

"I shall remember that," he promised. "It has been a long time since I visited your world." A look of anger spread across his face. "There are enough bizarre events happening right here in my own world. You were right about the war."

"Of course I was. Only someone who was as wrapped up in his work as you were could have missed it."

"Thank you," he said sardonically.

"May I see what you are working on now, before Gala returns?" asked Jinx.

"It will shock you," said Dali.

"If I wasn't shocked by *Un Chien Andalou*, or by your pornographic sketches—yes, I found them in one of your notebooks—I won't be shocked by this."

"It is not entirely finished," said Dali.

"That didn't stop you from showing me *The Persistence of Memory* every day when you were working on it."

He sighed. "All right. Come into the studio."

She followed him through the living room to the studio. There was a cloth hanging over the easel, obscuring the canvas.

"It has two titles," he announced.

"Two?"

He nodded. "My first inclination was to call it *Premonitions of Civil War*. Then I decided that was too direct, too accurate a description for a Dali painting, so I am also calling it *Soft Construction With Baked Beans*."

She laughed aloud. "That hardly sounds like a painting that will shock me."

"It will shock everyone when I am done with it."

He pulled back the cloth, revealing the half-finished painting. It was very clearly a Dali painting, yet it was different. Atop all the surrealistic structures was the most hideous face Jinx had ever seen, atop a pile of dismembered bodies and their entrails. She stared at it and shuddered.

"It isn't suffering," she said at last. "It seems to be almost happy."

"It is the spirit of war," answered Dali. "It revels in death and destruction. That is another reason I have given it a second title: it may be inspired by the Spanish Civil War, but it is the hideous spirit of *all* wars."

"You were right," said Jinx. "It *is* frightening."

"It is supposed to be."

"When will it be done?"

"I don't know," he replied. "I may wait another year, perhaps even two, to finish it. I need to distance myself from the war to properly represent it. I had to get that face on canvas, but the rest can wait."

"Not for long," said Jinx. "Not if you stay here."

"It's the *Spanish* Civil War, not the French," said Dali.

She sighed. "How can you be such a genius in some ways, and so uninformed in others?"

"Are we expecting a French Civil War?" he asked. "I thought they had that in 1789."

"There will be war, and Paris will almost certainly fall, but it will not be a civil war. In fact, it will be a world war."

"A world war?" he asked, puzzled.

"A war fought by all the nations of the world—or almost all."

"Like the Great War?"

"Worse."

"Let me guess," said Dali. "You think it will be caused by that German painter."

She nodded. "And others. Mostly by him."

"What is going on?" he mused. "How did the world come to be even more bizarre than my paintings?"

CHAPTER 15

Big Town

Dali found a copy of *The New Yorker* in his studio. He picked it up, thumbed through it, and tossed it in a corner, then went back to painting.

A few minutes later, Gala entered the room.

"Where is the magazine?" she asked.

Dali shrugged and pointed to it.

"What is it doing there?" she demanded.

"It was in the way."

"But I wanted you to read it!"

"The whole thing?" he asked distastefully.

"Look at the material toward the front," she said. "All the theater, all the art exhibits, the hundreds of elegant restaurants. Look at the ads for Saks and Brooks Brothers."

"Why must I look?"

"It seems a sophisticated and interesting city," she replied. "It is filled with precisely the kind of people we need to meet."

"All seven million of them?" said Dali.

"Spare me your feeble attempts at humor. I think we should take a trip to America."

"Well, we would be farther from that crazy German painter," said Dali.

"We would meet people of wealth and breeding, people with money."

"I thought America was responsible for the Depression. Are you suggesting that it is no longer suffering from it?"

"Not every American is poor and hungry," answered Gala. "And most of those who aren't are living in New York."

"Fine," said Dali. "Now, what's the *real* reason?"

"We need money. You need to expand your audience, and we need to expand our social circle."

"I thought we were making so much money we could barely count it," said Dali, frowning.

"We made some poor investments, and some of the exchange rates on the sales of your paintings were very usurious. New York is filled with expensive art galleries and rich patrons."

"And you base this conclusion upon reading one issue of *The New Yorker*?" he asked. "Are you sure it's accurate?"

"Certainly," answered Gala. "It has a worldwide reputation."

"So does the little German," said Dali.

Gala's face hardened. "We're going, and that's that."

And that was that. Almost.

They had enough for third-class passage on a less than top-of-the-line steamship, but they would have reached America without a penny. Dali refused to ask any of his friends for money, but somehow Gala got word to Pablo Picasso, who sent them a gift of five hundred dollars.

"This is dreadful!" said Dali upon hearing the news. "How can I ever face him again?"

"It is wonderful," she corrected him. "Now we can go where there is fresh money, where people will pay to see you."

"You mean to see my paintings."

"I mean what I said," she replied. "I have hired an agent to arrange a series of lectures for you."

"But my English is very poor!"

"You'll have two weeks to practice it aboard the ship," she said with a total lack of concern.

"How long will we be there?" asked Dali.

"I haven't decided," answered Gala.

"What you are trying to say is that we don't have return fare," said Dali accusingly.

"Don't worry about it," said Gala. "Your job is painting. Mine is paying the bills."

He could tell that further discussion was fruitless, so he sighed and began packing.

The trip was dull and uneventful. Dali kept opening his closet whenever Gala was out on the deck, hoping to find a door to Jinx's world in the back, but there was nothing but the bulkhead. He took to sitting alone in the bar at three in the morning, hoping Jinx would sense that Gala was asleep and show up so he could voice his concerns about the trip to her.

Well, he thought on his last night at sea, trying to ignore his disappointment, *she's got her own life to live. Besides, if I entered her world without her to guide me, I'd never find my way back out.*

They docked in the morning, and a few moments later they were in a taxi, heading to their hotel. Dali was stunned by the size, the sheer *energy,* of the city. London had been as big, but nothing he'd ever experienced was as vibrant.

He felt small and lost, but Gala was in her element. She dragged him to one social function after another. He was so annoyed at having to attend that his behavior was more aberrant than usual—but his reputation had preceded him and everyone *expected* him to act like a mad artist.

He gave his lectures and found that he enjoyed the power he had over his audience. After all, he knew what he was trying to say, but he mangled the language so much that they had to pay close attention in order to understand him. And at least once each lecture, he'd pull something out of his pocket—a mouse, a snake, *something*—and treat it like a pet to give them something further to talk about when they spoke to their friends of the lecture.

Gala convinced a few galleries to display his work, and in the first week alone he sold twelve paintings for more than five thousand dollars at a time when the average American was making fifteen dollars a week. He wanted to send Picasso his five hundred dollars, but he had never learned how to write a check, and Gala wouldn't let him mail cash.

The first thing Gala did with the money was move them to better quarters—a suite at the Waldorf Astoria. After the bellhop had brought their luggage to the room and waited for Gala to tip him, she announced that she was going out to wrangle an invitation to a very posh party the next night.

Dali waited until she'd been gone for five minutes—long enough to make sure she wasn't coming back for something she'd forgotten—and then opened the door to the walk-in closet in the bedroom. Sure enough, there was the door to Jinx's world.

He didn't want to enter it alone, so instead he opened it in the hope she would see it. He sat down on an easy chair to wait for her. Belatedly it occurred to him that one of the stranger and more dangerous creatures he'd seen in her world could simply walk through the door into the Waldorf suite. He got up to close the door, but just as he got to his feet Jinx stepped through it.

"Hello, Salvador," she said. "I am so glad to see that you've moved to America. It's the safest place to be." Suddenly, she smiled. "Well, except for Antarctica."

"We're returning to France the day after tomorrow," said Dali.

"That is foolish. Can't you see what's going to happen?"

"That's for politicians and generals to worry about," he replied. "My only concern is my painting."

"I would think a major concern would be to live long enough to keep on painting."

"If you're just here to argue, forget it," said Dali. "Gala does it better."

"No," she said. "I am here to show you a painting I am very proud of, and to get your honest opinion."

"Then I shall be happy to evaluate it for you," said Dali. "Where is it?"

"I'll get it," she said. "I wasn't sure you'd be here."

She walked back through the door to her own world, then returned a moment later with a small canvas in her hand.

"All right," said Dali. "Let me see it."

She handed it to him. He took it, glanced at it, frowned, and studied it carefully.

"Why did you choose to paint Gala?" he asked at last.

"*You* paint her all the time," answered Jinx. "Why shouldn't I?"

"Because you are not married to her."

"Have you never painted anyone you are not married to?"

"You have done a very fine, very naturalistic painting of her," said Dali, still frowning. "But why does she appear so harsh? Why those lines in her face? Why the hint of a sneer about her lips? Have you ever seen her look like this?"

"No. It is merely the way I imagine her."

"Well, it is all wrong."

"That's why I am here," she said, handing him a charcoal. "Show me how to correct it."

Dali took the charcoal, seemed about to draw a line, paused, thought better of it, held the charcoal above another part of the painting, considered it again, then finally sighed and handed both the charcoal and the painting back to her.

"I was mistaken," he said. "It requires no improvement. That is the way she looks—from time to time, anyway."

"Thank you."

"You are becoming quite good, you know."

"I have a good teacher," said Jinx. "I wish he had enough brains not to return to Europe."

"The Spanish Civil War took place in my homeland," explained Dali, "but what is going on in Europe doesn't concern me. I am a noncombatant."

"I don't think bullets and bombs differentiate between combatants and noncombatants."

"France possesses the Maginot Line, the most impenetrable military defense in the world, and England possesses a fleet second to none. Mussolini has made Italy's trains run on time." said Dali. "I think you are being an alarmist. There is no cause for worry."

"I've been studying American history since you came here," said Jinx. "I'll bet America's General Custer said those very words right before he reached the Little Big Horn."

CHAPTER 16

Alternatives

The world didn't get any safer. Dali and Gala moved to France, then to Mussolini's Italy. They didn't stay long in either place, and finally they fled to the United States to sit out the war in relative comfort.

They took up residence in Virginia, where Dali kept turning out paintings. Some were brilliant, more weren't, but all of them bore his distinctive touch and all sold, some for truly outrageous prices.

Gala kept up all her society contacts, and encouraged Dali to behave even more outrageously, which served to make him even more of a celebrity—and if there was one thing Americans loved, it was a celebrity. After all, Gala explained, far more Americans admired Babe Ruth and Billy the Kid than Walt Whitman and Henry David Thoreau, and Dali's wildly eccentric behavior, some of it legitimate, much of it staged, proved that she was right.

As for Dali himself, he was reasonably happy. He had his safety, he had his painting, he had his celebrity, he was making money even faster than Gala could spend it—and he had his closet.

He didn't visit it very often any more, but he was always happy to see

Jinx, who still seemed not to have aged since the day he first met her. Her visits were few and far between, but whenever they were together they discussed art. In fact, while Dali lectured on art to anyone who would pay his exorbitant fees, and pontificated on it to members of the worshipful press, he found that he never actually *discussed* it with anyone except Jinx.

"What about Gala?" asked Jinx one afternoon when Dali made mention of the fact.

"She discusses how to get the best price for my art, and how to make me even more famous, but she never actually talks about art with me," said Dali. "Do you know that after I agreed to paint one of her friend's portraits, she told him I would add a burning giraffe for another ten thousand dollars?"

"Did you agree?" asked Jinx, curious.

"Not at first."

"But finally?"

Dali grimaced at the memory. "Gala has her own methods of persuasion."

"I'm sorry."

"There are two sides to every issue," responded Dali. "If it weren't for Gala, no one would want a Dali portrait with or without a burning giraffe." He decided to change the subject. "You haven't mentioned my mustache lately," he said, stroking it gently with his fingertips. "How do you like it?"

"It looks like the ends are vines reaching to the sky," answered Jinx. "It is very distinctive."

"I don't think there is another like it anywhere in the world," said Dali with a touch of pride.

"I think you're probably right," said Jinx.

There was an uneasy silence.

"Would you like some tea?" asked Dali after a moment. "Or better still, a Coke or a Pepsi?"

"What is a Coke or a Pepsi?" she asked, puzzled.

"Uniquely American drinks. I have some of each in the icebox."

"There's no alcohol in them?"

"None."

"All right, I'll have one."

"I'll be right back," he said, heading off to the kitchen. He returned a moment later with a twelve-ounce bottle in each hand and handed one to her.

"I like it," said Jinx, after taking a taste. "By the way, where is your latest work? I couldn't find any new canvases."

"I am expanding my repertoire," he announced.

"What do you mean?"

"Have you ever seen a moving picture?"

"I saw *Un Chien Andalou.*"

"They have progressed enormously since then. Now they have words and music."

"You mean like a play where everyone sings and dances?" she asked.

"Well, they can do that, too," he said. "But for the most part, the moving pictures use music for background and emphasis. And one of the greatest directors is a man named Alfred Hitchcock."

"You are making a movie?"

"Not exactly," said Dali, making no attempt to hide his excitement. "But Hitchcock is making a film titled *Spellbound*, about a man who might or might not be insane…"

"Based on you?" she asked.

"No," he said. "Though it would make a better story if it was. Anyway, the film will show this man's fantasies and delusions, and I am designing the sets for that part of it. It is very exciting."

"How long will it take you?"

He shrugged. "I have never done it before, so I don't know. Maybe half a year, maybe a little longer."

"That's between five and ten paintings you won't do, Salvador," she pointed out.

"I know," he said. "But I think my best work as a painter is behind me. I need to expand, to move into other fields, fields that my genius has not touched yet."

"You are a painter, Salvador," insisted Jinx. "You should paint."

"I am an *artist*," he replied. "I should create art. I can create it on canvas, but I am also learning to create it on photographic plates, and Hitchcock has hired me to create it on celluloid."

"Time is very elastic in my world," said Jinx, "but it is fixed and rigid in yours. One second in Virginia is exactly the same duration as one second in Spain or Italy. Time is the one commodity you cannot replace, so it is the one commodity you cannot afford to waste."

"I am not wasting my time," he said defensively. "I am expanding my horizons."

"You are the man who created *The Persistence of Memory* and *The Inventions of the Monsters* and all the others. How much further can your horizons expand?"

"I don't know," he admitted. "But I have almost reached my creative limit as a painter. It is time to apply my talents in other directions."

"I think you are making a mistake."

"You are just a girl."

"Have I ever misled you before?" said Jinx.

He stared at her thoughtfully. "No," he said at last. "No, you have not."

"I am not misleading you now," said Jinx, walking back to the door in the back of the closet. "Will you at least think about it?"

"I promise you," said Dali as she returned to her own world. "I will consider it."

CHAPTER 17

Antidotes

He thought about it, as he promised he would, but he decided to continue his association with the cinema, and Gala was of course thrilled to be making new contacts among the Hollywood elite.

Jack Warner took time off from battling with his headstrong stars, Humphrey Bogart and Bette Davis, to commission a portrait by Dali, and to introduce him to a number of powerful Hollywood executives. The friendship ended when Dali delivered his portrait. Warner ordered him to repaint one of his hands and the wall behind him, and Dali explained in no uncertain terms that Warner could edit all the Warner Brothers films he wanted, but that no one edited a Dali portrait.

One of the men Warner had introduced him to was fascinated by his art and his ideas, and that man was Walt Disney. Disney wanted to collaborate with Dali on a cartoon, not one for children but something with artistic ambitions such as his earlier *Fantasia*. Dali moved to California and showed up every morning at the studio, bubbling over with new ideas and dozens of drawings each day—but eventually Disney lost interest and dropped the project.

Dali painted almost nothing after the end of World War II. When he wasn't courting Hollywood or letting Hollywood court him, he dabbled again in photography, he began writing scores of articles and even completed his autobiography, and—with Gala's urging and direction—he perfected his performance art decades before the term "performance art" came into being.

Soon almost all of his time was occupied with merely being Salvador Dali for a public that couldn't get enough of the half-crazed painter with the unique mustache. His output of paintings diminished, nothing he created for Hollywood except *Spellbound* was actually made, and he proved to be far less brilliant as a photographer than as a painter.

He took a new interest in religion, and combined it with an old interest in Gala. Whenever he painted the Virgin Mary, or any female saint, she almost always bore Gala's face. Before long even the critics who had fallen in love with his work were finding it a little too predictable.

He was sitting alone in his studio on a September evening—Gala spent less and less time with him, and more and more time among her Hollywood and socialite friends—and he was reading yet another review suggesting that the madman of Spain had lost his touch, that perhaps he was becoming too sane to create the kind of work that had captivated the world for close to twenty years.

"That's a very cruel review, and not at all accurate," said a familiar voice, and he turned to see Jinx standing behind him, reading the review over his shoulder.

"The man is right," said Dali unhappily. "I have lost whatever I had. I took surrealism as far as it could be taken. It was not a dead end, but there is nothing further that I can do with it except repeat myself."

"Well?" said Jinx.

"Well what?" he replied irritably.

"Who says you have to keep being a surrealist?"

"What are you talking about?" demanded Dali. "You *live* in a surreal world."

"It is not surreal to me," she said. "But that is neither here nor there. You are a supremely talented painter. If you feel you have gone as far as you can in one direction, then perhaps it is time to go in another."

"In *what* direction?" he said. "Am I to paint happy children and loving grandparents and thoughtful doctors? Norman Rockwell is already doing that. Should the great Dali stoop to painting the covers for pulp magazines?"

"Of course not," answered Jinx. "Although I would love to see what you would do with a science fiction magazine. No, the choice is not between copying Norman Rockwell and painting pulp covers, and you know it."

"Yes, I know it," he said unhappily. "But I sit before a canvas, and I am lost. I know what I must not paint, but I don't know what I *should* paint. Take yourself, young Jinx. Toulouse-Lautrec would paint you one way, Picasso another, Magritte a third, even Norman Rockwell would paint you in his own distinctive manner. But the only distinctive style I have is surrealism, and I am sick of it."

"You'll think of something," she said.

"I doubt it."

"Of course you will," she said encouragingly. "How did you come to surrealism?"

"My friend Freud," answered Dali. "And you, of course. But he's been dead for years, and even if he were here he would just tell me to paint what my subconscious says to paint, and you are unable to suggest any alternative."

"Then perhaps you will have to find another Freud," offered Jinx.

He frowned. "Another Freud? You mean another student of the mind, like Jung?"

"Probably not," she said. "You've plundered your subconscious for twenty years now. It's time to find a way to lock it off, and open other doors."

He studied her intently. "What have you in mind?"

"Nothing. *I* am not unhappy with my art."

"I will not let you off that easily," he insisted. "You know something. What is it?"

"I?" she said innocently. "*I* am not in search of an antidote to Sigmund Freud."

"An antidote?" he asked, and considered the notion. "An antidote," he repeated, a hint of excitement creeping into his voice. "Yes, that might be the answer: an antidote to Sigmund Freud."

Suddenly, Dali got to his feet and entered the closet. At first Jinx thought he was going to enter her world again, but instead he grabbed his satin cloak and silver-headed cane and came back out.

"Where are you going?" she asked.

"The world is my pharmacy," he announced. "Somewhere in it I will find the antidote I seek."

CHAPTER 18

Heisenberg

*P*ortraits, thought Dali, as he walked down the street. *No one expects anything special from portraits. In fact, when I try to give them something special, as I did with Jack Warner, they object. I suppose I can keep doing portraits while hunting for this antidote.*

He stopped at a corner newsstand, where he noticed a poster for a speech being given that night by Werner Heisenberg. Dali checked his watch. He had time to get to the auditorium, and who would make a better subject for the great Salvador Dali than the creator of quantum mechanics and Heisenberg's Uncertainty Principle?

Uncertainty Principle, he mused. *It even sounds like a Dali painting.*

He walked the six blocks to the auditorium. The manager recognized him instantly and insisted that Dali be his guest, bowing obsequiously and escorting the artist to the front of the audience, where he was offered a seat in the first row. Dali couldn't remember whether he was supposed to tip managers as well as waiters and cab drivers, but before he could decide, the manager was gone.

He could hear the whispers in the audience behind him. "It's Dali!"

"No it isn't!" "It must be. Look at the mustache!" "But doesn't he live in Spain?" "Go ask him!" "*You* go ask him!" Dali could have spent the whole evening contentedly sitting there with his back to the audience, listening to the awed whispering, but then the lights went down and an announcer came out, explaining that the greatest theoretical physicist since Albert Einstein was about to speak.

A moment later, Heisenberg came onstage. He began with a joke that elicited polite, rather than enthusiastic, laughter, and then quickly moved into the body of his speech, most of which dealt with quantum mechanics and went right over the audience's head.

But not Dali's.

He didn't understand most of what he heard, but he understood that this man was the polar opposite of Freud. If it couldn't be proved, Heisenberg didn't believe in it. If something wasn't logical, then it was clearly wrong and just as clearly worthless.

The more he spoke, the more excited Dali became. He hadn't felt like this since that first day he had encountered Freud. Freud had opened a door for him, had shown him the power of his psyche, of his dreams and fears and longings. Heisenberg clearly had no use for such things. Dreams were something men were meant to outgrow, fears were to be overcome, longings were to be approached in the most logical manner.

This man could be my salvation!

The speech lasted for ninety minutes. By the end, more than half the audience had left, and the man sitting right behind Dali was snoring gently, but Dali sat as if mesmerized. Finally he got to his feet, applauding wildly, and the remaining members of the audience were shamed into giving Heisenberg a standing ovation.

Then, as Heisenberg was walking off the stage, Dali raced up to him.

"I must speak to you!" he said excitedly.

"You are Salvador Dali, are you not?" asked Heisenberg, peering at him through thick glasses.

"Yes."

"I have long admired your mastery of your technique, your use of color and perspective," said Heisenberg. "I do not pretend to understand your subject matter, but then, I don't imagine you understand mine either."

"But I want to!"

"The great surrealist?" said Heisenberg with an amused smile. "Now, that *is* interesting."

"When can we speak together?" asked Dali.

"There is a charming bar in my hotel. They have provided me with a chauffeur and a limousine, so why don't you join me, and he will drive us both there."

Dali eagerly agreed, and a few minutes later they were sitting in the bar, awaiting their drinks.

"I was surprised to see you in the audience, Señor Dali," Heisenberg was saying. "This is the seventh city on my tour, and mostly what I get are mathematics and physics professors. I am quite flattered to have an artist of your reputation attend one of my lectures."

"I will be honest with you, Dr. Heisenberg…" began Dali.

"Call me Werner."

"And you may call me Salvador," replied Dali. "I will be honest with you, Werner. I did not come to hear your lecture. At least, not initially. I came to see if I wanted to paint your portrait, and to see if you would like to commission it—but you have opened my eyes. The portrait, if you will pose for it, will be yours for free."

"You make more from one painting than I make in a year of lecturing," said Heisenberg. "Surely my lecture wasn't *that* interesting."

"It was not your lecture," replied Dali. "It was *you*, Werner."

Heisenberg frowned. "I do not understand, Señor Dali."

"Salvador, please," Dali corrected him.

"I understand your name," replied Heisenberg. "I do not understand your motives."

The waiter arrived with their brandies. Dali had no idea what to pay him, or indeed which of the two men should pay. Then he decided that since he was the supplicant, the obligation was his, so he pulled a bill out of his pocket and handed it to the waiter. The young man tucked it in his pocket and began walking away.

"He'll want change," Heisenberg called after him.

"I will?" asked Dali.

"About eighteen dollars' worth," said Heisenberg, staring at him curiously.

"How much are the drinks?"

"It is a fine brandy," said Heisenberg, as if explaining it to a child, "so they cost a dollar apiece. You gave him a twenty-dollar bill."

"And I will get change from that?"

"Are you quite sure that *I* am the man you wish to see?" asked Heisenberg.

"Yes," said Dali. "I sense that you are my antidote."

"I beg your pardon?" replied Heisenberg, looking at Dali as if he might start foaming at the mouth any second.

"You are the counterbalance to Freud."

"*Sigmund* Freud?"

Dali nodded. "It was he who opened the door to surrealism for me. Now I need someone to close that door, to lead me down another path, to substitute logic for the irrationality in my paintings."

"This may be a request beyond my poor powers," said Heisenberg. "The irrationality lies within you, Salvador. I really don't see how I can eradicate it."

"What if I were to show you, to *prove* to you, that I am not mad and not irrational," said Dali, "that I actually paint what I see?"

"I would say you are more desperately in need of help than I thought—and not the kind of help that I am capable of giving to you."

Dali smiled. "That is a very good answer, Werner."

"It pleases you that I cannot help you?"

"Oh, you can help me," replied Dali happily. "It pleases me that you do not believe me, that you insist everything must be logical and rational. If you did not, then indeed you would be unable to help me."

"I suppose it will not surprise you to know that I have absolutely no idea what you are talking about," said Heisenberg.

"But you will," said Dali. "We are going to become friends, you and I."

Dali unfolded his paper cocktail napkin, pulled out a pencil, and began sketching his companion's face.

"I have always admired such a skill," said Heisenberg, as Dali's hand moved faster and faster. "Doubtless because I have a total lack of skill in that area. Poor manual dexterity, poor hand-eye coordination. Given time I could create a mathematically precise representation of you, but"—he sighed—"it would not be art."

"Have you never had the desire to express what you *feel* rather than what you see?"

"Of course," said Heisenberg. "I have expressed my horror at the Nazis, my love for my wife, my admiration for—"

"That is verbally," Dali interrupted him. "Have you no desire to express it any other way?"

"As I said, I am totally without skill in all areas of art," answered Heisenberg, "and I have yet to discover a formula or lemma that expresses emotion."

"Yes, Werner," said Dali decisively, "you are just the man for me. I can't believe I found you so soon after talking with…with my friend." He put his pencil away and shoved the finished sketch across the table to Heisenberg, who picked it up and studied it.

"It is an excellent likeness," said Heisenberg. "May I keep it?"

"Of course."

Heisenberg handed the sketch back to Dali. "Would you sign it, please? Otherwise no one will believe that I own an original Dali."

"You will own a better one, done in oils, before the summer is out," Dali promised as he signed the napkin and returned it to Heisenberg, who folded it neatly and inserted it in a breast pocket.

"But I have performed no service for you, nor based on what you've said will I be able to," protested Heisenberg.

"I don't know if you will be able to, either," admitted Dali. "But I know that if anyone can, you are the man."

"I still don't know what you want."

"I want to close a certain door and open others," said Dali. He lowered his voice. "The problem is, I don't know if the door is real."

"Well, here we have the basic difference between realism and surrealism," said Heisenberg. "I would say that a door is real or it is not. You would say that it is possibly or occasionally real."

"We really are not in disagreement," said Dali. "If it's real, it is always real." He paused. "I just don't know if it is. But *if* it is, you must teach me how to keep it locked."

"With a key, of course."

"This is a unique door, and it will require a unique key, one that I suspect only you can supply."

"This is all very interesting, Salvador, but it is late, I am getting tired, and you keep speaking in riddles. Perhaps you will lay out the problem in terms a realist like myself can understand?"

"You will think me crazy."

"I already do," said Heisenberg with a smile. "Are you?"

Dali shrugged. "I don't know."

"Well, you must either tell me what this is all about or let the subject drop. I am through trying to guess what you are getting at."

"What would you say if I told you that there is another world," began Dali, "a world where the most amazing things occur, where cause often follows effect, where many of the things I've painted actually exist?"

"I would say that you have an overactive imagination," answered

Heisenberg. "But of course, it is that imagination that has helped make you world-famous."

"What if I told you I paint what I see, not what I imagine?"

"I would not believe you," said Heisenberg. "Although," he added thoughtfully, "I suppose it is possible that *you* believe it."

"Very good," said Dali. He leaned forward suddenly, almost knocking over his brandy. "What if I told you I could take you there?"

"To this world you are talking about?"

"Yes."

"I would not believe it."

"I have a final question, friend Werner," said Dali.

"Then ask it."

"Will you humor me and let me try to show you this world? I will still paint your portrait, regardless of what happens."

Heisenberg stared at him for a long moment, then shrugged and smiled. "All right," he said. "Where is your spaceship?"

Dali returned his smile. "In my studio."

Heisenberg's expression said it all: *The man is as crazy as a loon.*

"Gala—my wife—will not be home for another three hours," continued Dali. "Can your driver take us there now? By tomorrow you may have second thoughts."

"I have second thoughts right now," said Heisenberg. "But you seem harmless enough. I do have a question, though. Why can your wife not be present?"

"I do not share this world with her."

"So no one else knows about it except you?"

"One person does," replied Dali.

"Who?"

"You will meet her," said Dali. *Unless I am truly insane, which is somewhere between possible and probable.*

"All right," said Heisenberg, getting to his feet. "Let's get this over with. And you do not have to paint my portrait for free. I cannot hold a madman to such a promise."

"Wait two hours and then tell me if I am still a madman."

They went out to the limo and awoke the chauffeur, who had been napping in the front seat, and reached Dali's house in ten minutes.

"Wait for me here, Bernard," said Heisenberg to the chauffeur. "I suspect I will not be very long."

"Yes, sir."

Dali unlocked the front door, turned on a light in the foyer, waited for Heisenberg to enter, and then closed the door behind him.

"Where is it?" asked Heisenberg.

"Follow me," said Dali, leading him to the studio.

"I see no spaceship here."

"It is not a ship, but a portal to another world," replied Dali.

"And where is this portal?"

"In the back of the closet."

Heisenberg gave him a look of total disbelief. "The back of the closet?"

Dali nodded. "Yes."

"All right," said Heisenberg with a sigh. "I've come this far. Another few feet can't hurt."

"Right this way," said Dali, walking into the closet. He moved aside all the things he had piled there to hide the door from Gala. "Do you see this door?"

"Yes," said Heisenberg.

"Open it."

"You're sure this doesn't lead to the attic?"

"If it does, you'll know it soon enough."

Heisenberg shrugged, opened the door, and stepped through.

CHAPTER 19

Disintegration

Dali stood beside Heisenberg, surveying the world he had come to know so well. Here was the purple mucous swamp, there the forest of singing trees, off in the distance the herd of talking burning giraffes. He looked around for Jinx and was surprised that he didn't see her.

"Well?" asked Dali. "What do you think now, friend Werner?"

"It's an attic," said Heisenberg.

"You are joking!" exclaimed Dali.

"It's an attic," repeated Heisenberg.

Dali scanned the landscape. "Look!" he said, pointing. "Do you not see the lion with the face of the beautiful woman?"

"I am sorry, Salvador," said Heisenberg, "but what I see are rafters."

And as the word left his mouth, the lion vanished.

"No!" cried Dali. "It is a trick of the sunlight!"

Heisenberg stared at him sympathetically. "There is no sunlight, Salvador. There is no light at all, except that which is coming from your studio."

"Look there!" said Dali, pointing. "Surely you can see the forest! The trees are singing, and all their limbs are human arms! It is as plain as day."

"Salvador, we are in an attic," said Heisenberg. "There is no forest."

And the forest disappeared.

"This can't be happening!" shouted Dali desperately. "I am not imagining these things! Look, Werner! Forget the animals. You *must* see the weeping castle on the hill!"

"No."

"Look harder. It's windows are eyes, and tears roll down its walls."

"I wish I could see it, Salvador, but I cannot."

The weeping castle vanished.

Dali began shaking uncontrollably. *How can this be? I often said I was insane, but until this instant I never believed it!*

His eyes narrowed. *If I don't suggest it, if I don't tell him what's there, maybe then he can't tell me what's not there.*

Dali looked down at the swirling golden grass that had paused briefly in its migration between empty pasturelands. "What are we standing on?" he said.

"A wooden floor. Why?"

The grass disappeared.

No! I didn't say we were on grass! How can you vanish if he doesn't deny I see you?

Dali swayed dizzily, and Heisenberg put an arm around him to support him.

"You're not well, Salvador. Let me take you back into your studio. You need to sit down."

Dali looked ahead, and saw Jinx coming over a hill, waving at him.

Oh, my God! Go away! Don't let him not see you!

He weakly held up a hand, as if to stop her physically, though she was still a quarter mile away.

"What is it?" asked Heisenberg.

I can't tell you, or you'll make her vanish. We've got to get back to my world before you guess that she's here, and then she won't be. I can't let you reason her out of existence!

"The studio!" he gasped. "Please hurry!"

"Yes, of course," said Heisenberg, helping him turn and half-carrying him back to the studio.

"The door!" mumbled Dali. "Close it."

Heisenberg did so, and a moment later Dali sat, exhausted, on his chair.

"Can I get you anything, Salvador?" asked Heisenberg. "A cold compress? Or perhaps some cognac?"

"No, Werner," said Dali. "I will be all right in a moment."

"You had me worried there."

"You really saw nothing?"

Heisenberg shook his head. "No." He stared at Dali. "And you really did?"

"I thought I did. I must be as crazy as they say I am."

"Perhaps."

"And now you are humoring me."

"Not really," said Heisenberg. "There is an old saying that in the country of the blind, the one-eyed man is king. Perhaps those of us who are not artists are blind in a way. What you saw was not real to me, but that doesn't mean it wasn't real to you."

"You are being kind," said Dali, "but if it is only real to me, then it is not real at all."

"I am a scientist. I believe what I see, what I can prove. You are an artist; you believe what you can imagine. I saw an attic. I believe there is nothing there but an attic. But if what you saw could inspire work such as *The Persistence of Memory*, then I would call it a fine madness, and I would do nothing to cure it."

Dali shook his head. "I asked you here to show me how to eradicate the world behind the closet—except that when you did, I was overwhelmed by horror and regret."

"When I did *what*?"

"Every time you couldn't see something I pointed to, it disappeared," said Dali. "The experience was shattering, first because it means I am truly mad, and second because I had not realized the destruction of my dream world would be so painful."

"Perhaps you are seeking to destroy the wrong thing," said Heisenberg.

"What are you suggesting?" asked Dali.

"That you do not want to put a world, whether real or imaginary, to death, but to write *fini* to your own romance with surrealism."

"Yes, of course—but how?" asked Dali, confused.

"Your greatest painting is *The Persistence of Memory*, is it not?"

"Yes."

"You created it," continued Heisenberg. "Perhaps it is time to un-create it."

"Are you suggesting I sneak into the museum and destroy the canvas?"

Heisenberg shook his head. "There are thousands of prints. It has been reproduced in numerous books. Destroying the original will alter nothing, nor prepare you for the next step in your artistic evolution."

"Then I don't understand what you are suggesting."

"If you think about it, you will," said Heisenberg. "And now I must take my leave of you." He walked to the door, stopped, and turned back to Dali. "I pledge to you that I will mention this episode to no one. I think it would be best if you would do the same."

Then he was gone.

CHAPTER 20

Resurrection

It took Dali almost an hour to regain his composure. Then he picked up a print of *The Persistence of Memory* and began wondering how he could possibly un-create a work he had already painted.

Well, let me see, he thought, picking up a pencil. *Heisenberg is a mathematician and a scientist. He lives in a precise world, so of course he would see the painting as part of that world. He wouldn't make it vanish, because that would be an act of magic and not of science. So to un-create it, he would show, in precise mathematical terms, exactly how it was created. Those soft forms, those rounded shapes, would be broken down to their molecular level and then slowly begin disintegrating, showing the lines along which they were seamlessly joined.*

He began drawing over the print, and his excitement grew. *If I do this and this, if I do not change the subject matter, but turn it from surrealism into science…*

By morning, he knew exactly what he wanted to do, and that day he began work on *The Disintegration of the Persistence of Memory*. It took Dali, who had once turned out paintings in days, even hours, two years to finish it, but when he was done he knew it would be generally acknowledged to be his greatest painting in almost two decades.

The day it was completed, Dali should have felt elated. He knew what he had accomplished, but he was overwhelmed by a bittersweet regret — not for surrealism, which he had (he hoped) grown beyond, but because he would never see Jinx again. He missed her smile, her curiosity, even her criticism. He hoped she was happy in her world, which he would never visit again, and that she was still working at her painting.

He took Gala out to dinner to celebrate finishing the painting and listened with glazed eyes as she listed all the people she wanted him to meet and all the things she wanted to buy. Afterward, they returned to the seaside villa he had bought her on Spain's Port Lligat.

Gala was tired and went directly to bed, but Dali was restless. He walked into his studio, took another look at *The Disintegration of the Persistence of Memory*, then went out onto the patio that overlooked the water.

I should be elated, he thought. *Why do I feel this sense of loss?*

He looked out at the water, watching the moonlight reflecting off the gentle ripples.

"It is a very good painting," said a soft voice from behind him.

He turned to see a familiar redheaded face.

"I was afraid I would never see you again," he said, keeping his voice low so as not to wake Gala.

"You can't get rid of me that easily, my old friend," said Jinx. "We still have work to do."

"Yes," said Dali, feeling enormously relieved. "Yes, we do."

"And we will do it together," she continued. "You should never have invited your friend to my world. He couldn't understand."

"No, he couldn't," agreed Dali.

"From now on, it will be just the two of us," said Jinx.

"Just the two of us," he promised happily.

"And great things lie ahead," she said.

"Great things," echoed Dali, feeling complete again.

Dali's Life and Art

He was born Salvador Felipe Jacinto Dali i Domenech on May 11, 1904, in the small Spanish farm community of Figueres. But he was not the first Salvador Dali born to his parents. He had been preceded by a brother of the same name, who died at twenty-one months of age. Probably because he bore the name, Dali grew up feeling that he was a substitute and was driven to prove his own worth.

He showed artistic talent early on. He was only fourteen years old when he had his first small exhibit, and twenty-one when he had a major exhibit in Barcelona after attending Madrid's San Fernando Academy of Fine Arts.

His fame was limited to Spain until 1928, when three of his paintings were displayed in the third annual Carnegie International Exhibition in Pittsburgh. He held a one-man show in Paris in 1929, joined the Paris Surrealist Group, and met and fell in love with Gala Eluard, the wife of the French poet Paul Eluard. Gala soon became his lover, his business manager, and frequently his inspiration and model. They were married in a civil ceremony in 1934.

Dali had been acknowledged as the greatest surrealist painter in the world with the creation of *The Persistence of Memory*. But he had no interest in politics and clashed with the other members of the surrealistic movement, who wanted his paintings to reflect their political views. They actually held a trial in 1934, and expelled him from the movement, which was absolutely ludicrous, since in his own words and the public's opinion, "Le Surrealisme c'est moi!"

Still, by 1940 he felt he had carried surrealism as far as he could, and was looking for new challenges. He found some of them in Hollywood after he and Gala fled to America to escape World War II, and while he labored at cinema, photography, writing, and etching, Gala made sure the public was aware of his flamboyance, booking him into any venue that would have him, and encouraging the public display of the most bizarre aspects of his personality.

After returning to his beloved Port Lligat after the war, Dali also returned to the Catholic faith he had abandoned as a young man, and he and Gala were married (or remarried) in a religious ceremony in Spain in 1958.

Two Dali museums opened during his lifetime, one in Spain and another in Florida, and the prices paid for his paintings soared to astronomical levels.

Gala died in 1982, and Dali's health began to fade immediately thereafter. He was badly burned in a fire in 1984, he had a pacemaker inserted in 1986, and he finally died of heart failure in a Spanish hospital on January 23, 1989.

His art practically defines surrealism. An absolute master of technique and perspective, Dali pulled images out of his mind, bizarre images that no one had seen before, but that nonetheless struck a responsive chord.

His most famous work was unquestionably *The Persistence of Memory*, and rare is the book collecting Dali's art that does not also include *The Disintegration of the Persistence of Memory*, the two forming a

twenty-three-year Moebius trip through surrealism that brought him back
to the imagine that brought him his greatest fame.

Dali put Gala in dozens of his paintings. Less often mentioned is the
fact that he also put exceptionally strange and bizarre versions of himself in
many paintings as well. His images of the Spanish Civil War (*Soft
Construction with Boiled Beans*), of Jesus looking down from a cosmic
cross at the Virgin Mary as represented by Gala (*Crucifixion*), of an elephant on enormous stilt-like legs (*The Space Elephant*)…well, nothing like
these things had ever been seen. And like much of Dali's best work, once
seen could never be forgotten. His standing in the world of art? Well,
Picasso will probably always be considered the greatest and most famous
artist of the twentieth century, but a strong case could be made for Dali as
the runner-up in both categories. And when you come to surrealism, his
primacy is assured. There is Dali, and there is everyone else. It's really as
simple as that.

A Time Line of Salvador Dali's Life

1904   Salvador Dali is born in Figueres, Spain on May 11.

1918   Dali has his first exhibition at age fourteen.

1922   Dali attends the San Fernando Royal Academy of Fine Arts in Madrid.

1925   Dali has his first major exhibition in Barcelona.

1927   Dali is called up for nine months of military service.

1929   Dali meets Gala Eluard, and joins the surrealist movement.

1931   *The Persistence of Memory*.

1934   Dali marries Gala in a civil ceremony on January 30.

1936   *Soft Construction with Boiled Beans: Premonition of Civil War*.

1940   Dali and Gala flee Paris and settle in America for the next eight years, dividing their time between New York and California. Dali not only paints, but works with Alfred Hitchcock on *Spellbound* and with Walt Disney on a cartoon project.

1942   Dali's autobiography, *The Secret Life of Salvador Dali*, is published.

1944   Dali, who is painting less and expanding into other fields, publishes his first novel, *Rostras Oscuras*.

1948   Dali and Gala return to Spain, though Dali continues to spend each winter in New York.

1952–54   *The Disintegration of the Persistence of Memory.*

1958   Dali and Gala marry in a religious ceremony in Girona, Spain.

1974   The Teatre-Museu Dali, a museum devoted to Dali's work, opens in Figueres, Spain.

1982   The Dali Museum opens in St. Petersburg, Florida. Gala dies on June 10. King Juan Carlos of Spain makes Dali the Marquis of Pubol.

1989   Dali dies of heart failure on January 23 in Figueres, and is buried at the Teatre-Museu Dali.

For More Information

Biography:

The Persistence of Memory, by Meredith Etherington-Smith (Da Capo Press, 1995)

Autobiography:

The Secret Life of Dali, by Salvador Dali (Dover, 1993)

Criticism:

Dali and Postmodernism, by Mark J. Lafountain (State University of New York, 1997)

Art books:

Dali: The Paintings, by Gilles Neret and Robert Descharnes (Taschen, 2001)

Dali, by Dawn Ades (Rizzoli, 2004)

Dali: The Salvador Dali Museum Collection, by Robert S. Lubar
   (Bullfinch, 2000)

Original art on display:

The Teatre-Museu Dali, Figueres, Spain
The Dali Museum, St. Petersburg, Florida

Web sites:

http://en.wikipedia.org/wiki/SalvadorDali/
http://www.virtualdali.com/
http://www.daliweb.tampa.fl.us/
http://www.artcyclopedia.com/artists/dalisalvador.html
http://www.artchive.com/artchive/D/dali.html
http://www.seven7.demon.co.uk/dali/